★

The air was still and I was sweating as I neared the rim of the scarp where the ground leveled off. Here, mesquite and acacia, nourished by the spring, grew thick and dense. The opening was so narrow that the goats must have passed through in single file to reach the precious water. I had to duck and put one arm across my face to keep the thorns from scratching. Still hunched, I hesitated for an instant, then shoved through the overgrowth and straightened up.

From out of the quivering grasses surrounding the muddy pool, dozens of vultures lumbered into flight. As their beating wings stirred the air, I was overwhelmed by the stench of death.

★

DEATH OF A HEALING WOMAN

ALLANA MARTIN

WORLDWIDE.

TORONTO • NEW YORK • LONDON
AMSTERDAM • PARIS • SYDNEY • HAMBURG
STOCKHOLM • ATHENS • TOKYO • MILAN
MADRID • WARSAW • BUDAPEST • AUCKLAND

To James

DEATH OF A HEALING WOMAN

A Worldwide Mystery/August 1998

First published by St. Martin's Press, Incorporated.

ISBN 0-373-26281-7

Thanks are due the following people for providing information for this book: With the Texas Department of Health, Susan Neal, Ph.D., supervisor, Medical Virology Branch, Bureau of Laboratories, and James Wright, Regional Zoonosis Veterinarian. To Kevin Buchanan, DVM, Jodi Overton, veterinary assistant, and K. D. Dorris, DVM.

After the Conquest, and as the old Aztec priests died off and were not replaced, isolated native groups had difficulty maintaining the complex Aztec pantheon. In the absence of a formally trained priest, the shaman *(curandero)* became an agent of cultural preservation.

—Bernard Ortiz de Montellano,
Folk Medicine: The Art and Science

ONE

WE FEAR DEATH, my friend Maria had told me, so we laugh at it, and adorn it in gaudy colors, and give it shape in the form of macabre candies in order to hide our fear and make death palatable.

It was *El Día de los Muertos,* the Day of the Dead, and I had brought flowers for the graves of Maria and her husband.

I jammed the marigolds into the vases angrily. I was angry because I had yet to come to terms with their deaths. Angry because I resented Andalon's easy assumption that their murders were a part of the necessary violence of minor drug lords. Angry because I wanted answers. No. I wanted more. I wanted justice. I wanted retribution. I wanted revenge.

To achieve any one of those required that the killer be known, and in the six months since Maria and Bill had been shot at point-blank range, their bodies doused with gasoline and set aflame, neither a hint of the motive for the killings nor the identity of the killer had surfaced.

The odds of my winning the lottery with my dollar-a-week investment were greater than the chances of my tasting sweet revenge. So I told myself to calm down and tried to arrange the bright yellow flowers into more seemly bunches.

Aztec custom specified yellow for adults. I knew that Maria would have approved of this symbolic veneration of her Spanish-Indian ancestry. And Bill would have liked anything that made his wife happy. I touched my fingertips to the cool stones, running them across the incised names: Maria Elena Ortega-Deed, William August Deed.

Something bumped me hard from behind. As I stretched out a hand to steady myself a child squealed, and the weight lifted off my back. I turned my head and saw a young woman holding tightly to the arm of a wriggling little boy. She gave me an apologetic look as she dusted him off and led him back to the family plot.

The small adobe-walled cemetery was crowded with families from both sides of the border. Old men and women, some dressed in somber black, washed the dust from the white-washed crosses and *sillar* block tombs and rearranged the circles of stones that kept evil spirits at bay. Younger adults pulled weeds, hauled water, painted, and repaired, while their children ran in and out among the graves, excited by the holiday atmosphere and the feast to come, with skull-shaped candies and brightly tinted *pan de muerto,* the sweet bread that would entice the dead back to the living world on this night between the first and second of November.

I got to my feet and stared down at the grave of my best friend. Born on the border and bilingual, Maria and I had shared the giddy secrets of childhood, teenage anxieties, and adult confidences, worries, and joys. I had taken for granted that we would grow old in friendship, would reminisce, and would bore one another with stories about grandchildren. I had assumed too much.

Trying to shake off my blue mood, I took comfort in the explosion of noise and people and color around me. Flowers had been heaped on each grave. Wreaths of mint marigold, coffee cans stuffed with the velvety purple spikes of bush sage, and fragrant bouquets of pineapple sage turned the graves into extravagant altars. Later the cemetery would glow with hundreds of candles lighted for the all-night vigil. Feeling more at peace, I knelt and broke off one of the marigold blossoms and fixed it in a buttonhole of my blouse for remembrance.

"Who's minding the store, Texana?"

I smiled at the soft voice and turned around. Annie Luna's voice always makes me smile. It's so deceptive, with a hint of hesitancy and shyness, which doesn't exist at all in the personality of the strong-minded twenty-five-year-old. Annie is tiny, maybe five-foot-one and ninety pounds. She was wearing jeans and a turquoise shirt. Her waist-length hair had been pulled back and braided in a businesslike fashion. I liked Annie and was actively promoting the growth of a dormant romance between her and Billy Deed, Maria's son.

"Cadillac Charlie is in charge," I explained.

Annie glanced at the Deed graves.

"Billy will like those flowers," she said. The smile on her face did not reach her eyes. A nurse at the VA hospital in San Antonio, Annie had come home to help care for her mother, who was dying slowly of cancer. Annie looked so miserable that I volunteered the information she probably had joined me to get.

"Billy's taking a prisoner to Marfa. He stopped to

help a man change a flat. Turned out the man didn't have a spare, a license, or a registration slip for the car. What the poor mule did have was a five-pound bag of marijuana taped under the front bumper. Billy thought he'd make it back for the vigil.''

Annie shrugged, trying for uninterest and reminding me how glad I was not to be young and in love with someone I considered the wrong man.

Annie tugged at her braid and changed the subject.

"My father asks if you'd like to share our meal later.''

As in all small communities, our knowledge of each other's activities and personal habits is intimate and instant. The Lunas knew that Clay had left early to drive to Sul Ross University to speak at a seminar on controlling rabies in the border counties and that I would be alone for the evening. I appreciated the thoughtfulness of the invitation, but explained to Annie that I'd be away, too.

"I'm going to see Rhea Fair.''

Annie cocked her head and dropped her eyes, masking a curiosity she was too polite to show. I saw no reason not to tell her why I was going to see the *curandera.*

"Rhea's a week overdue picking up her supplies. She doesn't buy much at a time, so she should be running out by now. I'm taking a few things out to her.''

Annie frowned. "I hope she's not sick.'' She paused. "I wonder why she didn't send Trinidad.''

"He may not be on this side of the river right now,'' I suggested, though in truth I had wondered the same thing. Trinidad Quiroz had worked for the

Fairs when Rhea's husband Jake had been alive, and
the old man had remained loyal to the widow. Once
a month, Trinidad would drive Rhea in his ancient
pickup to get her supplies. White Dog, Rhea's current pet, a mongrel of uneven temperament, rode in
the bed of the pickup, pacing from side to side, jumping down to hide underneath as soon as the pickup
stopped.

"Mrs. Fair is a good person," Annie said, twisting
the end of her braid around her finger. "I hope nothing's wrong."

"I wouldn't worry," I told her. "She had a visitor
last week. A young woman. She stopped at the store
and bought some beans and bread and asked for directions to the Fair place. That's probably why Rhea
hasn't been in to shop for herself." It was general
knowledge that the *curandera* never accepted payment for the herbal remedies that she blended and
handed out so freely, so many visitors took food as
a gift.

"Her reputation as a healing woman must be
growing," Annie said. "I hear she's had people
come all the way from El Paso for her remedies."

I nodded. "The woman who stopped last week
was driving a rental Suburban. She'd gotten it in Alpine." I dug in the pocket of my jeans for my keys.
"I'd better get moving."

"If you feel like it, on your way back stop for the
vigil," Annie said. "It's my favorite part of the
day."

She turned to go back to her family. I headed toward the gates and my pickup, working my way

along the crowded aisles and nodding and speaking briefly to old friends.

A few latecomers came in at the gates as I left. I climbed behind the wheel, started the motor, and pulled onto the road. There was no other traffic.

The cemetery sits on a rise at the southeastern tip of El Polvo. Heading northwest, I passed the one-room school and the post office, and then the double line of flat-roofed adobes and the scattering of trailer homes that make up the rest of the town. As I speeded up, a half dozen mutts chased after the pickup, barking in mock ferocity before wheeling back to the shade.

The blacktop lasts only as far as the edge of town; there it turns into a lava-rock surface that has to be driven with a careful hand on the wheel because of the 15 percent grade. The road parallels the Rio Grande as the river snakes its way between Texas and Mexico, a thin line of murky blue bounded by the gray-green of salt cedar.

Five miles farther and the road disappears altogether as the fractured buttes and pinnacles of ancient lava flows close in on either side. The river is diminished here to a shallow humble sheet of water. You can drive across the riverbed to where the road picks up in Mexico, a lifeline connecting distant villages and solitary adobes.

I turned the pickup away from the river crossing and toward the blue of the Chinati mountains. Ahead, startled by the noise, a roadrunner chasing a lizard leaped over his quarry and lifted off in a low glide.

Mindful of the pickup's shocks, I slowed to a crawl as the track crossed the loose stones of a dry creek and wound on through creosote bush, clumps of yucca, and spikes of sotol. Here and there the rimrock fanned out in waves, and the track climbed steadily.

Three winding miles and two cattleguards farther, I pulled over and parked. The rest of the way had to be made on foot, following a rocky path as it climbed the mesa for a quarter mile. I lifted out the box of tightly packed supplies from the bed of the pickup. I had brought bags of rice and beans, a loaf of bread, two jars of peanut butter and one of jelly, five pounds of coffee, paper towels, and a can of kerosene.

Starting up the path, I almost fell. I had caught my foot in a mesh bag on the ground, the kind illegals often use to carry a jug of water, tins of sardines, and bread. Our section of the river, roughly sixty miles or so, is a trickle of dirty water known only to smugglers, a few ranchers, and a handful of border patrol agents. Illegals, deceived by the ease of getting across the border, and without a compass or any knowledge of the terrain that lies ahead, cross over only to die of snakebite or dehydration or sunstroke in the high desert mountains, their bodies bleached to white bone before they are found months later by cowhands checking for strays.

I shook my foot free of the mesh bag and wished safe journey to the man who had carried it.

Slightly out of breath, I reached the end of the path, a mesa where the land had been cleared of brush and cacti for perhaps an acre. In the center of the clearing stood Rhea Fair's house, built of cotton-wood poles chinked with cement and roofed with used tin, so that both the scarce rain and the abundant sunlight leaked through the old nail holes.

I put down the box and stood catching my breath, puzzled by the empty clearing. Where were the rangy hens scratching in the dirt? The wormy goats browsing the edges of the brush? Why no White Dog barking and jumping at the end of his tether? The only living thing I could see was a redtail hawk high above, gliding on the breathy air.

"Rhea," I called.

Keeer-r-r… cried the hawk.

Rhea was shy and liked time to make herself tidy before coming to the door, so I waited, turning to face the horizon, expecting to hear her ask me in. The view in front of me was a grand sweep of the river valley across to the sepia hills of Mexico's Sierra Bonita range, but I paid little attention to the vista. Instead, I listened. What I didn't hear worried me. No muted sounds from within the thin-walled house. No bleating of goats from the distant brush. No sound at all save the rush of an immense silence.

I approached the house and hesitated near the door, a sagging screen held together by graying wood.

"Rhea, it's Texana Jones."

Shading my eyes with cupped hands, I put my nose to the screen and peered inside. I could see the dim interior of the long narrow room. An acrid smell like a dead campfire made me wrinkle my nose.

I yanked open the screen and stepped inside, stopping to let my eyes adjust from the intense sun. Stacks of old newspapers and magazines lined the walls, making the room seem smaller than it was. I made my way around Rhea's sunken armchair and past the wooden table, its bright blue top nearly hidden by large jars of dried herbs, to the woodstove. I felt its surface. Cold. Rhea had not cooked this morning. When I glanced at the zinc-topped counter, my heart constricted. On the drain beside the sink lay a five-pound bag of dried pinto beans and a loaf of bread. The groceries the young woman had bought from me the week before were untouched. I could see through the wrapper that the bread had molded in the heat.

Frightened now, I turned to the doorway leading into the only other room. I more than half expected to find Rhea lying on the floor, dead from a stroke or heart attack. Instead, I found the source of the scorched odor. Someone had set fire to the bedclothes. A blackened pile covered the bed. The flames had consumed all but the edges of a patchwork quilt and bits of stuffing from the cotton mattress. Ashes had fallen through the bedsprings and onto the dirt floor. Soot marred the walls and ceiling and dripped from a cobweb in the corner.

The room was tiny, and I had to edge my way around the iron bed to reach the one window. Trying to let in more light, I wiped the cloudy pane with the palm of my hand, but succeeded only in smearing the oily residue. I gave up, wiped my hand on my pants, and felt the bedstead. Cool. So were the ashes. The bedclothes had burned hours, perhaps days, ago.

Then I saw that more than bedclothes had been burned. A chunk of charred wood had caught in the springs. I stretched my arm to reach and shift the ashes on the floor beneath the bed and felt a sharp straight edge that on inspection turned out to be a melted metal picture frame with a few adhering lumps of what must have been glass.

Other than the bed, the room was bare. No bedside table, no shelf. No objects. In my few previous visits, I had never been in this second room, but I had no doubt that Rhea had some keepsakes—photos of her sons as children, surely, and of her husband Jake. Where were these things, if not burned? And who had burned them? And why? Had Rhea done this herself? I had known the isolation and hardships of desert life to turn habits into eccentricities, and eccentricities into madness.

Suddenly I felt the extent of my intrusion into Rhea's privacy. I wanted out of there, back into the sunlight. I jumped to my feet and whirled around, then froze, dazzled by a kaleidoscope of color that ran from floor to ceiling of the only interior wall. I had been so focused on the burned bedclothes that I had failed to notice the wall. From the blue of forget-me-nots to the yellow of daffodils, from tiny pictures to full pages, the wall had been papered with pictures of flowers cut from magazines. The glossy colors remained bright, untouched by the smoke, which had been drawn out the three exterior walls through the cracks in the chinking.

My eyes burned with tears. Here was the garden that Rhea could never grow in the harsh soil of the desert. The *curandera* had impressed me as remarkably stoic and self-sufficient, satisfied with the life she lived. This flower-covered wall revealed a wistful side to the woman that I had missed, a longing for options she did not have.

I shook my head. I hoped I was reading too much into Rhea's simple decorations, which might be nothing more than a love of color. I hurried back to the front room and made one more circuit, seeking a clue to what might have happened and where Rhea might be. I'd do better, I decided, to look around outside. Rhea might be lying somewhere with a broken leg.

I stood in the middle of the clearing and shouted her name.

Keeer-r-r... The hawk's strident cry mocked my own.

If I didn't find Rhea soon, I'd go for help. It would take planes and riders to search the brush. I scouted around the clearing, eyes to the ground, hoping to spot the imprint of Rhea's boots to give me some idea of a direction in which to search. But the packed ground revealed little—a few marks from the sharp hooves of the goats, an almost invisible print of the dog's paw, and plenty of dried goat droppings. Dried. Why none fresh?

I expanded my search into the brush around the clearing, working my way around islands of prickly pear. I found nothing except a few gummy clumps of chicken feathers. Going in further circles seemed futile. Time for me to get back to the pickup and let Billy Deed take over. After the murder of his parents he had run for constable and won. It would fall to him to organize a search for Rhea.

I spun around and realized that I'd lost my path through the prickly pear. I went in one direction, found myself walled in by cacti, backtracked, and tried again. After several attempts, I saw the print of my shoes in a sandy patch of ground and gradually

worked my way to a motte of second-growth mesquite I was sure I had passed before.

In the middle of the dense growth, a circle of grass
thrived, protected from the foraging goats by the
thorny shield. At its center the grass had been flattened in an oblong space of a little less than three
feet. The mark of a deer, perhaps, where it had bed-
ded down. Or the imprint of man curled into a fetal
position. I had seen such places in the brush before,
where a man, trembling with fear but with the courage born of a stubborn desperation, had lain all day,
hiding from searchers in the green uniforms of the
border patrol. In brush country you could walk
within inches of an illegal hiding in this way and
never catch a glimpse of him. The habit of stillness
is a virtue in the hunted, saving an animal's life,
allowing a man to elude capture.

I parted the mesquite limbs and leaned in to examine the crushed grass. I could see some kind of
dark discoloration flecking the blades. I went down
on my hands and knees, then to my stomach, and,
with a keen eye for snakes, wriggled my way in.
Rising to a squatting position, I shifted the grass and
saw clots of brown gathered at the base of a clump,
pooled when the blood had been fresh. From a
wounded animal, I told myself. The missing dog,
perhaps. For reasons I did not want to think about, I
reached behind my back and tugged free the handkerchief from the back pocket of my jeans, broke off
several of the splattered blades, and folded them in
the cloth, slipping it into the pocket again.

Wriggling backward, I cleared the mesquites and
got to my feet. I emptied the other back pocket, this

time pulling out a thick fold of toilet tissue. I tore off several sheets and impaled them on a mesquite thorn near the tip of a limb. If it turned out that the sheriff needed to see where I'd found the blood-splattered grass, I could tell him how I'd marked the spot.

I worked my roundabout way toward the house, my anxiety growing as I went. By the time I hit the clearing, I had broken into a run. Nearly at the trail, I tripped and went sprawling, scraping my hands and bruising both knees against the rocks. I rolled over and sat up, rubbing bits of dirt and grit out of my palms and glancing around for the cause of my fall.

It was a wooden stake, wedged sideways in the split of a large, low rock, the exposed tip of a buried boulder. It was the stake for White Dog's rope, the thick hemp knotted double to the wood. Normally the long stake was pounded into the hard earth by the front door of the house. White Dog must have pulled it free and dragged it to catch in the rock on this side of the clearing. The rope, dirty and worn, stretched across the ground, so much the color of the soil it was almost invisible.

I took the coarse hemp in my hand and followed it to the loose end. Untied, not cut or broken. So Rhea had let the dog free to roam for the night. But which night? And if she untied the dog, why was the stake pulled free? And where was White Dog? The last time I had been here, Rhea and White Dog had been out together, rounding up the goats to pen them for the night, protection against coyotes and the occasional mountain lion.

The goats. They watered at a spring somewhere in

the hills above the house. Rhea had told me how she collected water from the spring for the house, carrying it back in plastic jugs. I raised my eyes. In this region, a spring can be seen a long way off, an island of green in a brown landscape. I spotted it almost directly behind the house and halfway up the boulder-strewn mountainside. Now I had to locate the goats' path and follow it.

It lay to the right of the house, opposite the side where the rough privy stood, past the tin-and-board chicken coop and the sotol-fenced goat pen. I stopped at the coop long enough to be sure the chickens hadn't been locked up and forgotten. I knew the coop would be empty before I opened the door. If the chickens had been shut up, I'd have heard their hungry clucking halfway across the clearing. But I had to be sure. I hate the idea of any creature, even unlovable chickens, suffering.

My conscience clear about the fowls, I set my foot on the goats' path. An eerie sound made me freeze and sent a shiver of fear spiking up my spine. I waited, but the high, quivering note was not repeated. I turned slowly, eyes shifting to catch even a slight movement. I scanned the boulders, the pens, any place that could hide an animal.

"White Dog? Is that you?" I said tentatively, struggling to keep fear out of my voice. "Where are you, boy? Are you hurt?"

I eased in the direction from which I thought the sound had come, and, craning my head to see what might be hidden, I made my way toward the far side of the goats' circular pen, where the sotol shafts almost touched the upward thrust of rock as the small

mesa evolved into a higher, wider ridge. In the
shadow of the ridge, White Dog lay curled. His head
was up, but his red-rimmed eyes seemed unable to
focus on my moving figure. Though I could see no
visible sign of any wound, it was obvious that he
was in distress of some kind.

My every instinct said to reach out and pat the old
dog to comfort him. But fifteen years of being a vet's
wife, of listening to Clay's cautionary admonitions
to avoid the careless handling of any stray or sick
animal, stopped me. I could do nothing for the dog
now, and I had to check the spring for Rhea. White
Dog didn't look as if he planned on moving anytime
soon, so I backed away.

"I'll come back, boy, I promise," I told him, as
much to comfort myself as the dog.

More steep than the trail to the house, the goats'
path followed the line of least resistance in its indi-
rect route to the spring. As I reached a point where
the pale soil of the path curved around a solid rock
the size of a small house, a gleam of white caught
my eye. Two plastic milk jugs lay in a jumble of
fallen rock and prickly pear beside the path. I pic-
tured Rhea carrying the jugs to fill at the spring, and
I climbed faster.

The air was still and I was sweating as I neared
the rim of the scarp where the ground leveled off.
Here, mesquite and acacia, nourished by the spring,
grew thick and dense, the branches touching over the
tunnel-shaped opening the goats' persistent use had
made. The opening was so narrow that the goats must
have passed through in single file to reach the precious water. I had to duck and put one arm across

my face to keep the thorns from scratching, using the other hand to hold back branches.

As I wondered, half in irritation, why Rhea didn't trim the limbs, I heard the creaking flap of many wings. Still hunched, I hesitated for an instant, then shoved through the overgrowth and straightened up.

From out of the quivering grasses surrounding a muddy pool, dozens of vultures lumbered into flight. As their beating wings stirred the air, I was overwhelmed by the stench of death.

TWO

ABOVE THE POOL the vultures flapped and soared, rising on the hot currents of air in ever-widening circles.

I clamped a hand to my nose, swallowed my heart, and stepped from the encircling security of the trees. I had read somewhere that inhaling deeply and overloading the olfactory sense lessens the sick-making intensity of the smell of death. It didn't work, I reflected, as my stomach heaved.

The area around the pool extended in an oblong space of perhaps fifty by thirty feet. At the farthest narrow end the rock face sheered upward vertically. From a crevice in the wall of rock, an irregular ribbon of water ran into the pool. Holding my breath, I moved around the pool toward where the grass was flattened and torn.

I released my breath in gusty relief when I saw the carcass folded in the crushed grass was that of a goat. Within a few feet, I found three more dead goats. Or what was left of them, mostly bone and fur after the vultures had torn and dragged and feasted.

Vultures work fast. A couple of days, I thought, to do this. And Rhea's goats hadn't carried much flesh. What must have happened seemed obvious. As the goats came to the pool to drink, they had been caught, one or two at a time, by coyotes. I couldn't remember how many of the Spanish goats Rhea kept, but no more than five or six. The carcasses of the rest would be in the brush or farther up the mountainside. Rhea had loved the animals, had names for each, keeping them more for company than anything else.

If the goats had been left out to be hunted down by coyotes, it meant Rhea had been unable to pen them. The chickens vanished, probably carried off by hawks and owls, the goats dead, the dog cowering in hiding, Rhea missing. What had happened here? Could Rhea have gone somewhere with the young woman who had brought the groceries, thinking she would be back in time to pen the goats before dark? Had she fallen ill, unable to return home? I had no idea of Rhea's age, but I felt sure she was at least sixty, and she had not lived the easiest of lives. Had she suffered a heart attack or stroke and been driven to the hospital at Alpine or El Paso by her guest in the white Suburban?

Overhead the vultures, lulled by my stillness, closed their circles and swooped low, driving their shadows across the ground. I moved, and the vultures soared upward.

I skirted the pool. Its soft margins were scarred with the prints of birds, rodents, coyotes, skunks, and others, mixed and crisscrossed, joined by the ritual of thirst. At the pool's edge, a stout-bodied dragonfly, wings outstretched, rested on the tip of a reed. On the surface, water striders skimmed along in their ceaseless hunt for drowned insects. Below the surface, the pool itself was alive, deep green with algae.

My shoulders relaxed and my heart stopped its nervous pounding. I sighed almost contentedly in spite of the dead goats and glanced toward the source of all this abundant life, the spring.

And saw something white. A plastic milk jug.

Rhea was, in her way, tidy. And in her poverty, frugal. The jugs were utilitarian, used for carrying and storing the precious water. Never would she have discarded one here, or on the path where I had seen the other two. I moved closer on reluctant feet.

I stopped when I saw the toes of a pair of boots slanted up out of the tawny stems of needle grass. I felt as if my insides were disintegrating. In dread, I pressed my hand to my mouth and stepped closer.

After all, I had been right to be worried about Rhea. But if I had checked on her days earlier, I would not have saved her. She had been dead as long as the goats. Maybe longer. I took one step closer, saw her face, pivoted on my heel, and ran.

THREE

ARE YOU ALL RIGHT?'' Andalon asked me for the third time, concern showing on his square, kind face. And for the third time I nodded my reassurance, only this time I meant it. I could feel the blood circulating in my head again instead of down around my big toes, where it seemed to have sunk by the time I reached the Darke Ranch. Lank Carter, the ranch manager, had hurried out in response to my frantic honking and almost carried me from the pickup to the house.

It had taken me thirty minutes to drive the eight miles up the rough track to the Carters' house. It would probably have been faster to go back to El Polvo, but in my panic I had driven in the direction the pickup was pointed. Lank had plopped me down on the couch, called out to his wife Nora to fix coffee, and telephoned Andalon at the Presidio County sheriff's office in Marfa. That had been four hours ago. Nora had handed me a mug of coffee laced with whiskey and put her arm around my shoulders while I sipped it. I had never appreciated coffee or comfort more.

Andalon had made the two-and-a-half-hour drive in two hours flat. Now, Lank and the sheriff and I sat around the kitchen table, fresh coffee and pan-fried quail with scrambled eggs in front of us. Nora, a calm, quiet woman in a denim dress and comfortable shoes, stood at the gas range preparing more quail and eggs. Lank ate steadily, while Andalon chewed slowly, enjoying the succulent meat with the appreciation of a gourmet. I pushed the food around on my plate, my appetite left behind on the mesa with Rhea. Andalon had been to see the body before coming to interview me. Billy Deed and Deputy Dennis Bustamente were still there.

"I'd sure like to talk to Trinidad," Andalon was saying.

Lank stopped his coffee mug halfway to his lips.

"You don't think Trinidad shot her, do you?"

"Nothing to show that he did," Andalon said. "For that matter, I can't say for sure she was murdered until the autopsy. I could be wrong about the cause of death."

"You've done enough hunting and seen enough gunshot wounds to know, I'd say," Lank commented.

"Whoever killed her," Andalon said, "it sure wasn't for gain. Mrs. Fair had about as little as a human being can."

Lank looked down, embarrassed, as if he felt guilty for living in the home Rhea Fair had lost.

He needn't, I thought. Robert Drake, his boss, had paid Rhea three hundred thousand dollars, a fair price for the modest stone house and six thousand acres that was marginal forage even for goats. If Rhea's land had not joined Darke's thirty thousand acres, she'd have gotten less. I looked around the pleasant kitchen with its old-fashioned glass-fronted cabinets and tried to imagine Rhea cooking in here, her two sons doing their homework at the table, but failed. I had gone to school with the Fair boys, but the family had kept to themselves, and I had never visited in this house when Jake and Rhea had lived here.

Jake had been a ranch hand, working most of his adult life on the Triple Horn Ranch near Valentine. His brother had made a subsistence living on this place, and when he died of a ruptured gallbladder, Jake had inherited the property. That had been nearly twenty years ago. Four years later, Jake was dead. Six years after that, Rhea's sons, Matt and Luke, had got caught trying to smuggle cattle out of Mexico, and, on a tip, the DEA pulled up the floorboards of their trailer. They found cocaine. Rhea put up the ranch for bail, Matt and Luke fled to Mexico. So Rhea ended up with no money and no ranch.

"Do you think her sons have anything to do with Rhea's death?" I asked, saying aloud what I had been thinking.

Andalon shrugged. "It's possible. Matt and Luke are small-time troublemakers, just the kind that are too careless and too dumb to show the proper respect for the big players. I hear they're both holed up in Juarez. Matt's married to a Mexican national and runs a tourist shop selling cheap pottery and junk jewelry. Luke tends bar and shows tourists around for a fee. I'm sure both of 'em sell dope to any takers, but just street sales, not bulk."

"Some mule could have killed Mrs. Fair," Lank said. "We get too many of them carrying drugs through the ranch and going armed. I've had to tell the hands to carry a gun whenever they ride out."

I rubbed a hand across my eyes to keep the irritation from showing on my face. A year ago, Carlos

Suarez, a fourteen-year-old from El Polvo, had been dragged to death behind a pickup for holding back some marijuana for himself instead of making good his delivery. Ever since, everybody seemed ready to blame any violence on drug dealers or their mules, the men who moved the drugs across the border. They came on foot, or in old junk cars, like the man Billy Deed had arrested only that morning.

Andalon didn't need to see my face to know my feelings. I'd made them more than clear to him when he assumed that Maria and Bill Deed had been killed by a minor drug lord because they'd seen something they shouldn't have. Andalon seemed to think the fact that their bodies had been burned proved his assumption, but I'd told him anyone on the border knew drug lords often did such things, showing contempt for the corpse to intimidate the living. If the killer had wanted to make the deaths seem drug-related, gasoline was as easy to come by as guns. That was then. Now, Andalon gave me an almost apologetic glance before answering Lank's question.

"Ever since the border patrol launched Operation Blockade and shut down the crossings for a twenty-mile stretch at El Paso, we've had our hands full. Doesn't seem to matter that a man crossing the river in Presidio County will have to walk over some of the roughest land in the country for hundreds of miles before he gets to anyplace where he can find work. And the drug lords moved down, same as the illegals. You can't squeeze one without squeezing the other."

Lank nodded in vigorous agreement.

"'Bout a month ago, one of my men found a

three-hundred-pound calf, its throat cut and the carcass rough-butchered. Those folks from the other
side take what they need as they pass through.''

Andalon rubbed his chin and looked frustrated.

''In the past twelve months, the border patrol
picked up nearly three hundred thousand people
crossing the river illegally. And those are the numbers caught. Most are hard-working folks looking for
jobs. But there's lots of them come armed. My men
have had more armed confrontations in the past eighteen months—''

''You really think Rhea is another casualty of
some local drug war?'' I asked, interrupting Andalon
on his soapbox. I sympathized, but I didn't want to
hear the full speech. I'd heard it all after Maria and
Bill Deed had been murdered.

''War, I don't know. Skirmish is more likely,'' he
said. ''Mules and illegals like to follow the ranch
roads where they can, and the fact that the track past
Mrs. Fair's and straight through this place goes clear
to Highway 10 makes it very convenient. That mesh
bag you saw at the foot of the path to Mrs. Fair's
house could have been dropped anytime. I don't
think those things ever biodegrade. But for sure the
track is used by more than just the folks who live
out here.''

''Maybe Mrs. Fair caught someone taking water
at the spring and he killed her,'' Lank suggested.

''But why?'' I said. ''Rhea wouldn't have stopped
anyone getting water. None of us would. Out here,
that's like killing someone. Rhea knew what hardship
meant. She'd have given food or water to any illegal
who asked.''

Andalon looked at me, his eyes sad. "People kill for meanness sometimes."

"What about the visitor?" Lank asked. "This girl Texana says came by the trading post. What happened to her?"

"Probably she stopped, got some herbs or had a cleansing, and went on her way," Andalon said. He turned to me. "Too bad she paid you in cash instead of with a credit card. I'd already have a name and address. First thing tomorrow, I'll call up the car rental agency in Alpine and find out who she is. Good thing you noticed she drove a rental."

"You notice things like that when you're pumping gas," I said.

"Maybe the girl can help us narrow the time of death. It might take a while for the forensic people in San Antonio to get to the autopsy. We won't be on their priority list." He sighed.

"I've got plenty of food," Nora told Andalon, "if you want to take some back to your men. Coffee, too."

"Thanks, Nora," he said. "Billy and Dennis would sure appreciate a couple of sandwiches."

Nora immediately started to pack the sandwiches. I offered to help, but she shook her head and told me firmly to stay put. For the next few minutes, except for Nora's quiet movements, we sat unnaturally still, as if aware that our next actions would thrust us toward unknown events and irredeemable decisions and results.

Andalon broke our mutual reverie to remind me that he might need to talk with me again. Nora handed him a Thermos of hot coffee and the bag of sandwiches. She was pressing me to stay the night when a burst of voices and footsteps on the back porch interrupted her appeal.

The back door opened and four people in dusty pants and workshirts, their faces stained from too much sun, came halfway in and stopped, bunched in the doorway. The stocky man in front ran his fingers through thick red hair yellowing to white and turned inquisitive, intelligent eyes on us. Two young bearded men, distinguishable only by height, stared, curious and shy. The boyish young woman simply stood and looked tired, her eyes downcast.

I knew all of them to speak to. In the two years that Dr. Eliot Lofts, founder and director of the Lofts Research Foundation, had been excavating above Waller Creek on the Darke Ranch, the archaeologist and most of his various team members had been in the trading post to buy snacks and magazines. Robert Darke funded the project, providing room and board—a bunkhouse and Nora's cooking. Anything Lofts required, including frequent new team members, was flown in on Darke's private plane to the landing strip on the ranch. Present team members with Lofts were Kirk Anderson, the taller of the two men, Roy Hammit, and Mattie Brant, each a serious amateur who had paid three thousand dollars to spend a season, spring or fall, squatting to brush dirt and chip rock away from bits of bone and artifacts. And for the privilege of working with a man of such renown as Eliot Lofts.

"We can wait outside, Nora, if we're interrupting," Lofts said.

"No problem," Lank said. "We're running a little

behind, is all." He glanced at Andalon as if seeking approval, then hurriedly made introductions.

"I'd heard Mr. Darke had some high-powered scientists digging up bones and things on his place," Andalon said, rising to shake Lofts' hand. "Don't mind us. You folks sit on down."

I smiled at Andalon's folksy modesty. He always says being disarmingly country gets him more information than announcing his master's degree in psychology would.

"I don't know about high-powered, but digging up is right," Lofts said. "We've shifted tons of dirt with trowels."

Andalon acknowledged this with a smile, then said, "I'm looking into a death. Mrs. Fair—"

"The *curandera!*" Lofts said.

Andalon turned his intelligent eyes on the archaeologist. "Did you know her?" he asked.

Lofts nodded.

"If you folks don't mind putting off the nice meal Nora's got ready for you," Andalon said, "you could tell me what you know about her. I'd really appreciate any help you could give me with Mrs. Fair's sudden death."

"Of course, of course," Lofts said. He moved to the table and pulled out a chair.

Kirk and Roy eyed the platter of quail wistfully as they sat down. Mattie Brant looked somber.

Lofts said, "I heard of Mrs. Fair's remarkable reputation for healing and I sought her out. When traditional medicine has failed one, grasping at alternatives seems reasonable."

"And Mrs. Fair's herbs did the trick?" Andalon said.

"I've suffered from periodic agonizing headaches since childhood. I've tried everything. Biofeedback, prescription drugs and some not prescription, yoga, meditation. I could have completed three doctorates in the time I've spent trying to find a cure for the damnable pain."

"Mrs. Fair gave you something?" Andalon prompted.

"Fascinating woman," Lofts said. "Very compelling in her own quiet way. My first visit, she asked me to sit at that blue table. Blue is believed to be conducive to tranquillity, you know. Amazingly, before I had said a word about why I had come to see her, she told me. She said she could see the pain in my head and she put her hand right here."

Lofts placed his hand against his right temple.

A look passed among the team members. Obviously they had heard the story before.

"I was stunned," Lofts continued. "I could feel a tingling and a warmth moving through her hands and into my head. I felt simultaneously invigorated and relaxed. Then she took handfuls of herbs from one of several jars on the table and made up two preparations, one of rue and something she called *yerba de Cristo,* for a tea I was to drink each morning before breakfast. She gave me a second mix of herbs I was to take in the evening, stirring the powdered leaves into Mexican hot chocolate for, uh, cleansing my system, so to speak."

He smiled and added, "I admit, I believe she had

the power to heal in her hands. If pain could be cured by drinking an herbal tea, there'd be no sufferers."

Andalon said, "And you visited her more than once?"

"Yes."

"When did you last see her?"

Lofts didn't have to think over his answer.

"The twenty-fourth of last month, a Monday. I picked up a fresh supply of herbs."

"You seem very sure of the date," Andalon said.

"I detoured by Mrs. Fair's place on my way to keep an appointment with a colleague at the university in El Paso."

"Did you notice anything different about Mrs. Fair? Did she seem nervous? Worried? Sick?"

"She seemed quite as usual. Mrs. Fair didn't make small talk. A reticent woman, though perhaps that was only with me. She seemed very chatty with the man who was there when I arrived."

"Do you know who this man was?"

"No. He was a stranger to me. I thought perhaps he was a Mexican national because they were speaking Spanish as I walked up. Mrs. Fair didn't introduce us, and he left immediately. He had unusual eyes. Very wide set."

I looked at Andalon, but he turned his eyes to the other team members.

"Any of you," he asked, "visit the *curandera?*"

Mattie Brant said, "No." The two young men shook their heads.

Andalon nodded, thanked Lofts and the others for their patience, shook Lank's hand, and left. I said a hurried good night and followed at his heels. Behind me I could hear Lofts and his team throwing questions at Lank and Nora.

Andalon and I walked to where our vehicles stood on the drive under the intense illumination of a security light. Andalon stood beside me as I opened the door of my pickup and climbed in.

"You recognized the description of Mrs. Fair's visitor, didn't you?" he said.

"Of course. Matt Fair's the only man I know that has eyes so far apart he's never seen the centerline of the highway. I guess it's not too surprising that he'd come to visit his mother on the sly. It wasn't much of a risk; her place is so isolated. And from the other side, he could drive right up to the footbridge below the cutoff."

"When's the last time you knew Matt to be a dutiful son?"

"Never. Matt never did anything but stick out his hand and say 'Gimme.'"

"Yeah. Greed did seem to be his only motivation. You sure you can get home okay?"

I grinned and told him I felt better than I probably looked. Andalon and I are old friends. We went to high school together at Presidio. Andalon had been the school clown, fun and clever, and for a few months during my junior and his senior year we'd dated, deciding on friendship rather than love. After that, we'd looked out for each other, compared notes on those we dated, spent the long evenings of summer chasing the Marfa ghost lights and discussing our grandiose plans for the future.

Andalon turned to get into his vehicle.

"Wait," I cried, fishing in my pocket for the sample of bloodied grass. "I forgot to give you this," I told him, explaining where and how I'd found it.

Frowning, he gave me a look in which irritation warred with affection.

"Texana, if it was anyone else…"

"You'd humor me politely and throw the grass away."

He sighed and put the folded handkerchief into the pocket of his jacket.

"Let me know what you find out," I said.

He nodded and got in his pickup.

I let him pull out first and in the last light of day, I followed his pickup down the track until he pulled off.

I waved a hand at his retreating back as he started up the path to Rhea's house. As the sunlight faded, earth and sky lost form and definition, melding to a uniform bronze. As if at a signal, the voices of the coyotes rose from the falling dark, yips and howls that hovered in the air.

I shivered again, thought of the body on the mesa, and drove a little faster into the darkness ahead.

FOUR

NOT UNTIL I saw the flickering vigil lights as I passed the cemetery and began the last two-mile push toward home did I relax. And not until I drove across the graveled parking area and past the gas pumps in front of the trading post and saw the porch light shining on the big double doors did I feel safe.

I pulled around back, expecting to see Clay's pickup, but the only parked vehicle was Cadillac Charlie's 1955 white Fleetwood, its polished surface and shiny chrome reflecting my headlights.

Charlie mostly lives in and out of his car. Its trunk is equipped like a chuck wagon, with everything needed to camp under the stars, including a coffeepot, frying pan, Dutch oven, bedroll, and Coleman lamp. Thus prepared, Charlie travels both sides of the border, taking life as he finds it and odd jobs as offered. Charlie works for me a couple of times a year in exchange for gas and food. He unfurls his bedroll on the floor of the trading post and makes himself at home, reading books borrowed from my shelves until he falls asleep.

I nudged the pickup close to the back door and sat there, too drained of energy to move, relieved to be home. After a few minutes, I pushed open the door. My foot had just touched the ground when Clay wheeled in, driving like a policeman, gravel flying as he came to a quick stop beside my pickup.

At six-foot-one, my husband is four inches taller than I, straight and slim. His gray hair is thinning a little on top, and his features are strong: hooded eyes, prominent nose, firm mouth. He swung out of the pickup smiling at me, and my heart laid down its load.

"Hold this for me," he said, thrusting a white plastic-foam container the size of a hatbox at me.

"What is it?"

"The head of a coyote that probably had rabies."

He reached across the seat of the pickup for a thick stack of folders and a box of slides. The mention of the coyote penetrated the wall of my fatigue and jogged my memory.

"The dog," I wailed. "I forgot to tell Andalon about the dog."

"What dog?" Clay said.

He looked at me, registering my expression and goodness knows what else, slammed his pickup door shut, at the same time pushing mine closed with his foot, took my elbow, and guided me inside.

Our private quarters run the length of the trading post in a series of narrow rooms. I set the container with the coyote's head on the counter and collapsed into my rocking chair while Clay turned on lights and put his things away. When he came back, he had changed out of his suit into jeans and work shirt. He took the container from the counter and carried it into the pantry. I heard the big refrigerator door open and close. It's not every wife who has a coyote's head sitting beside the orange juice, but animal specimens must be kept cold.

I felt a kiss on top of my head and Clay's hand

patting my shoulder as he came around, tugged off my shoes, and wrapped my feet with a throw from the couch. I closed my eyes and let the tension seep away.

I kept awake by concentrating on the small sounds Clay made as he got out drinks: the flat pop of the liquor cabinet opening, the ring of the glasses touching, the gurgle of the bottle upending, and best of all, the footsteps bringing a glass my way.

I accepted the glass from his hand and sipped, letting the mellow flavor spread across my tongue and burst against the back of my throat. Not the green label, but the Crown Royal, a birthday present to Clay from my father. Ye gods, I must look awful, I thought, if Clay has to prime me with the good stuff.

He sat in the rocking chair across from mine, enjoying his whiskey. He asked no questions, made no effort to hurry me, but let me tell the story in my own way, which in this case, as tired and frazzled as I was, meant rambling sentences, digressions, a few tears, and much guilt about the dog.

When I was done, he got up and went to the kitchen refrigerator, rummaged until he found the leftover roast beef. While he cut transparent slices of onions and spread mayonnaise on the sourdough bread, he tried to reassure me.

"First thing in the morning, I'll check with Billy and find out if they found the dog. If not, I'll go up and see to it. If the animal's as sick as you say, he won't have gone anywhere. And if he's dead, it's not likely getting to him a few hours sooner would have saved him."

Clay handed me a plate, the thick sandwich on it

neatly cut in half. He settled in his recliner, balanced his plate on his knees, reached for the whiskey bottle, and recharged our glasses. Stimulated by the Crown Royal, I found enough appetite to eat half the sandwich. Clay finished his own and the rest of mine.

He collected our plates and glasses and took them to the sink to do the washing. I got up and lifted the dishtowel from its hook. Only when we had finished and were getting ready for bed did I finally remember to ask how the seminar had gone.

"Preaching to the converted's no trick," Clay said, sitting on the edge of the bed. "I did the usual show-and-tell with the slides."

"And when did you break away from the predictable?" I asked, knowing my iconoclastic husband.

He chuckled.

"As soon as all the big boys got there. Cassidy from the Department of Agriculture, Bales from the Centers for Disease Control, and Dade with the Department of Health. He'd just announced that A&M will have an oral vaccine for coyotes ready for February, and for foxes the following fall."

Dade is Dr. Brooks Dade, wildlife specialist and my husband's personal rival in the ongoing battle over how best to control rabies along the thousand-plus miles of border that coyotes and wild dogs cross at will and where the fight is a ceaseless holding action because of the prevalence of the disease in Mexico.

While I brushed my teeth, Clay finished his account of his day.

"I stood up and said we'd better be realistic and accept that rabies is spreading beyond our ability to

control it. When I said I advocated making strych-
nine or 1080 easily available to ranchers, the way the
poisons used to be, as the most practical way to slow
the disease, Old Dade got madder than a teased rattler."

"The animal rights people have hounded him," I
pointed out, but Clay dismissed that with a snort.

"If he thinks that's trouble, wait until the press
coverage when rabies moves north from the border
into a population center like San Antonio."

I asked Clay about the coyote's head.

"Anson Clark had it waiting for me at his gate.
He shot it when he drove to his mailbox. Anson said
it sat and watched him get out of his pickup and walk
up with the rifle without blinking. We needed an oral
vaccine drop *last* February."

"How can they hope to stop rabies with a vaccine
drop? I mean, this county is nearly four thousand
square miles."

"They can't," Clay said. "Either they'll hit the
counties with the highest rabies rates, or they'll go
for the ones closest to big population centers, which
means the Valley. At best, the disease is slowed, not
controlled. Certainly not eliminated."

Clay thrives on conflict. I could tell by his voice
that in spite of the setbacks, he had enjoyed the day.

"A vet from the Valley," he said, "told me about
a case in Laredo. One puppy exposed nineteen people to rabies. People think you have to be bitten, but
the virus can be transmitted through the mucous
membranes. A puppy licks a kid's face and some
saliva gets in the kid's eyes or nose. That's all it
takes."

He slipped his feet under the covers and sighed.

"I'm worn out with all this righteous indignation," he said.

I smiled, blessing the sense of humor that allowed him to keep things in perspective. Then I asked the question that had been on my mind since we'd been on the subject of rabies.

"Do you think White Dog might be rabid?"

"From what you described, the lethargy, his emaciated appearance, it could be he's in the last stages. You're sure you didn't touch him?"

"I'm sure."

Neither of us had to say what Clay feared most, that our ranching community faced a serious outbreak of the disease. An outbreak follows a pattern. An area would be clean, no sign of rabies. Rabid coyotes showed first, followed in a couple of weeks by symptoms in unvaccinated dogs. Within ten months, the area was besieged.

Besides his private practice, Clay serves, unsalaried, as the county vet, and as such he has pleaded, to no avail, for emergency mandatory pet vaccinations and the rounding up of stray animals.

Tired, but too wrought-up for sleep, we turned out the light and talked of Rhea's death. We tried, as people always do, to make sense of the senseless, to comfort ourselves with imagined explanations for a murderer among us. If each death diminishes us, how much more it diminishes the community in which it occurs. Ours is a community of few, spread over many miles, where isolation is paramount and interdependence a necessity. El Despoblado—the place without people—the Spanish called the area four hundred years ago. We seldom see our neighbors, but we know them well. We begrudge conformity and accept eccentricity. We remain self-contained, yet welcome strangers. The unexplained deaths last spring of Maria and Bill Deed and now Rhea Fair's death had disturbed our peace and assaulted our confidence. Murder had distanced us from one another in a way the miles never had.

FIVE

In the half-light of predawn Clay sat up in bed, swung his feet off the side, and crossed the room. He gathered his clothes and dressed in the bathroom, the door shut in order not to disturb me, a sentiment I much appreciated as I rolled over and snuggled down to sleep another hour.

When I emerged from the murky warmth of the bed, daylight glazed the far wall of the room and I squinted against the brightness. Thank goodness for Charlie, I thought, knowing he would have opened the doors for business promptly at 6 a.m. I showered and ran a brush through my hair, put on mascara, and dressed in slacks, shirt, and tennis shoes.

In the kitchen, I found a note from Clay reminding me to give the container with the coyote's head packed in ice to the UPS driver. I opened the refrigerator. Clay had addressed the container to the state's Department of Health laboratory in El Paso. There the technicians would determine whether it was a case of rabies.

The wall clock read 7:15. Luxuriating in Charlie's presence behind the front counter, I indulged in a second, then a third cup of coffee at the table in front of the kitchen window with its wide-angle view—tens of miles of the enfolding desert.

I am myself only here, in the borderland, *la frontera.* I had left this country for a year during a brief first marriage and had learned that I was out of step with the values by which much of the rest of the world judges happiness and success. I had fled back home, fearful that if I stayed away I might lose myself forever.

The border with Mexico is a boundary only in the minds of professional politicians in Washington. To *fronterizos* it is a country in itself, a country of the mind and soul, a place where two cultures grate and bleed and blend into a hybrid country, ambiguous, harsh, and full of extremes.

Even our language is different, a fluid mix of Spanish and English. Code-switching, the linguists call it when *fronterizos* move back and forth between Spanish to English in the same sentence. We call it *Tejano*.

My thoughts were intruded upon by someone in the front of the trading post hurling rapid-fire *Tejano* at Charlie, whose modulated tones punctuated the sound bites of a loud voice I recognized. I poured the remains of my coffee down the sink and pushed through the connecting door to say hello.

The log framing of the trading post dates from 1900. The floor-to-ceiling shelves are crowded with anything I think a customer may need and not want to make a hundred-mile drive to buy. That makes us a sort of combined general store, auto parts, farm and ranch, and hardware store. The place is big and lofty, and in this setting the little man across the counter from Charlie looked even smaller than he was.

I didn't think I'd made a sound coming in, but for a sedentary man Charlie seems to have a sixth-sense motion detector. He swiveled his plump body to face me and winked.

"Mr. Waites," he said, "is telling me what he needs in the way of supplies."

I wished Jesse Waites good morning and had to brace myself against his eardrum-blasting answer. Jesse is partially deaf, seldom speaks, and sounds angry when he does. Jesse lives alone, and likes it that way, up a canyon on the other side of the mesa from Rhea Fair's place. His home is a dulled silver trailer that rests like a giant tombstone on table-flat ground wedged between rock cliffs rising five hundred feet straight up on three sides.

Jesse tells the rare visitor to this site, mostly lost geologists or fossil hunters, that he got the trailer as a gift from an advertising agency for allowing them to drop it onto the site from a helicopter during the filming of a commercial. In truth, the trailer and nine hundred acres of mountainside belong to a doctor from Houston who, one especially fine spring, with the flood plains awash with flowers and the talus slopes misted with grass, had it set on skids and pulled up the canyon by a bulldozer. The doctor lasted halfway through the summer before abandoning his silver haven, leaving in such a hurry he left the door swinging open behind him. The following summer a ranch hand riding out in search of a mountain lion suspected of killing several calves passed the doctor's canyon and spied Jesse relaxing in a red leather recliner on a patch of grass beside the trailer. In the eight years that had gone by since, the doctor had never returned to claim his property, and Jesse had remained undisturbed.

Now I fed Jesse his favorite line.

"Did you hitch a ride this trip?"

I knew the answer would be yes. Impossible for him to have arrived so early by foot, his normal mode of transportation.

He cackled.

"Fooled that green kid good!"

The "green kid" referred to the fresh border patrol agent that Jesse had gulled into picking him up as an illegal. Brown and weathered as a vaquero and dressed in clothes stained and faded from long use, Jesse looks the part. And plays it up by walking with his head down and never raising a friendly hand at passing vehicles. Jesse starts his hike down the mesa at dawn. When he reaches Ranch Road 170, he walks the centerline with the measured stride of a man used to judging the distance to any destination in thousands of footsteps. Sooner or later a green 4 × 4 comes by checking the drag—a patch of cleared ground running beside the road and dragged smooth with a tire to show the footprints of illegals who cross over under the safety of darkness. Inevitably the driver, spotting Jesse, slows and pulls up beside him.

The border patrol agent, tanned arm propped in the open window, asks, "Are you from Mexico, señor?"

Jesse, head down to hide his blue gringo eyes, answers, "Sí," and shrugs when asked if he has his green card, agreeably allowing himself to be taken into custody. Of course, long before they reach the border patrol headquarters in Presidio, Jesse raises his eyes and brings out his ID.

Old hands in the federal agency consider Jesse's trick an initiation rite for the new boys. And there are plenty of those. Because of its climate and isolation, Presidio is considered a hardship station, and agents may ship out after two years.

"This 'un was sort of touchy," Jesse said.

"The agent came inside to ask if I could confirm that Mr. Waites was who he claimed to be," Charlie explained.

"Thought I'd killed some poor gringo for his wallet," Jesse said, grinning proudly at the unexpected bonus of his joke.

While we'd been talking, Charlie had packed coffee, lard, beans, flour, and sugar into the carryall in which Jesse totes his supplies. I added a box of 22's and asked Jesse if he needed anything else.

"I'm out of whiskey," he said.

Charlie went to the storeroom for a bottle. Jesse buys the cheapest brand, whether from necessity or because he likes his whiskey raw, I don't know. I wrapped the bottle Charlie handed me and put it into the carryall, cushioning it between the bags of sugar and flour, then totaled up the bill in the book. I run charge accounts for locals from both sides of the river.

Jesse moved away from the counter to prowl the aisles. He seemed to be looking for something and finally came to a stop in front of the glass-fronted refrigerator where I keep the vet supplies, mostly vaccines and antibiotics. He opened the unit's door, shifted the close-packed bottles and boluses, and made his selection. Coming back to the counter, he set down a brown glass bottle of penicillin solution.

"Need me a couple of needles and a syringe," he said.

I reached up to a nearby shelf and took down a box with various sizes of disposable syringes and needles of assorted gauges and lengths, suitable for doctoring everything from rabbits to bulls. Jesse picked out some of the smaller syringes, hesitated, and picked out four fine-gauged, plastic-capped needles.

I retotaled his bill and gave him his copy, which he carefully tucked away in a pocket.

"Heard about you finding Mrs. Fair," Jesse said. "Rough on you, I expect."

"Andalon thinks she was shot," I said, knowing that Jesse would know this already, probably having heard it from the border patrol agent, who would have learned about it from the sheriff's office. The border patrol had twenty-three employees operating out of Presidio, while Andalon had only three deputies, two in Marfa and one in Presidio. Numbers alone made it sensible for Andalon to keep the border patrol up to speed on what was happening, in the hopes that an agent might see something that would lead to an arrest.

Jesse said, "She was a good woman, Mrs. Fair."

After Jesse's stentorian tones, Charlie's gentle voice eased so softly into the conversation that his comment was half over before I listened.

"...that everything had its balance. She told me that God sent her the healing power as a means of helping her."

I don't know why it surprised me that Charlie knew Rhea, except that, thinking of it, I realized that

I had never heard him speak of her before. After the weather, gossip is the second-ranked subject of our conversation: the state of our health, who has had visitors, marriages and divorces, livestock sales. Gloom-and-doom political events in the rest of the world run a distant third.

After Jesse left, Charlie went back to taking inventory for me, and I worked the counter. I cashed paychecks for a couple of men who live on the other side of the river but work on this side, notarized divorce papers for a cowboy from one of the ranches, accepted a UPS delivery of beekeeping paraphernalia for a man who lives too far upriver to reach except, like Jesse, on foot, and sent the iced head of the coyote on its way to the lab. A score of people came in to talk about Rhea and hear from the horse's mouth how I found her. We ended up on the front porch drinking on-the-house sodas and beers while pondering Rhea's death and reminiscing about her life since she had come among us after marrying Jake Fair, a lifelong *fronterizo*. It was a nice memorial service and wake, done borderland style. The funeral, when it happened, would be briefer and less satisfactory. And though I drank only bottled water and listened with both ears, I heard nothing that might provide a motive for murder. Rhea had been liked and respected, and beyond her life with Jake Fair and her trouble with her sons, she was known as a very shy, private person.

At noon, Clay came in for lunch. He had driven to the line shack with Billy and Deputy Dennis Bustamente, whom Billy had put up for the night. They had found White Dog still cowering behind the goat pens, but in such bad shape that Clay had put the dog out of its misery immediately. Fearing rabies, he had removed the head and packed it for shipping as he had the coyote's. Dennis had offered to transport the specimen to Valentine on Highway 90 where the UPS driver could pick it up at a scheduled stop.

I thought about the dragged stake and rope I had tripped over. If White Dog had rabies, in the early stages of the disease he might have jerked the stake out of the ground in a nervous frenzy. And when the stake caught on the rock, either Rhea or Trinidad might have untied the rope from the animal's neck, not realizing the dog was sick. A perfect opportunity for the dog to bite or lick the person who loosed it.

Rabies may incubate in humans for as long as a year. It's preventable through vaccination, but fatal once it moves into nerve tissue. After a person is exposed, the sooner the vaccination shots are begun the better. By the time symptoms occur—nausea, depression, stomach pains, sore throat—it's too late.

I had to find Trinidad. If he'd been in contact with White Dog, he needed to begin rabies shots immediately, before it was too late for him.

SIX

A LOW CLOUD COVER spread between Valentine and Marfa, misting the distance in a soft gray, while over the Chinati mountains blue-black thunderheads rumbled, trailing streamers of rain and giving an illusion of coolness. Beyond Buckshot Rim the sky reflected clear blue, and the hot sun of late afternoon shone through the windshield and onto my face as I aimed the pickup toward Mexico. At the point where I drove across, the Rio Grande was barely a pickup-length wide and ankle deep.

On the Mexico side, the pickup lost traction, sending up a spray of fine sand before the wheels caught and carried me to the top of the bank, where I waved at a skinny boy leading a rough-coated burro down to drink in the murky, thin water.

Away from the river, I aimed the truck toward the hills along a well-defined track across cracked brown clay and pink talus. For the next half hour I held the speed to a bumper-to-bumper crawl. To go faster meant suffocating on dust as the vehicle bounced over irrigation ditches and across arroyos.

Clay had intended to come with me to reason with Trinidad, but a last-minute call on his office number ended that plan. As he grabbed his jacket and headed out the door, he managed to yell over his shoulder that if the heifer had wire in her stomach, he'd be late. I would have enjoyed his company, but I didn't mind making the drive alone. The desert encourages solitude. Outsiders who see this land and call it empty don't know the landscape intimately.

As I pulled up in front of the low fence that enclosed the yard of Trinidad Quiroz's adobe, a plump toddler made a bowlegged escape from the shade of the *sombra* and ran toward the pickup. A slim young woman in a wrap skirt and T-shirt caught the baby and scooped him up in her arms. She smiled at me and opened the gate as I got out.

"*Hola,* Florinda," I said, handing her a small paper bag. She greeted me shyly, avoiding eye contact, and led me into the shade of the *latillas*-roofed outdoor room.

I like the Quiroz home. Trinidad built it himself from bricks made on the site. The original house had two rooms, with a separate kitchen beneath a sotol arbor. Over the years a wing had been added, one room at a time, to accommodate three sons and five daughters. All the children were grown now, with children of their own, and Trinidad had family living on both sides of the border. After Trinidad's wife died, his youngest son, Joe, and Joe's wife Cordelia had moved home. Together, Joe and Trinidad herded 240 goats and 40 mules. Florinda is Joe's youngest daughter, living here while her husband works on a ranch in North Texas, managing the long journey home only twice a year.

Florinda put the baby down in the middle of a blanket spread on the stone floor, rolled a wooden ball toward him, and invited me to sit down. The baby's black eyes focused briefly on the toy, then shifted in a blink at the rustling of the paper bag.

Florinda removed the wrapper from a piece of candy. The baby wobbled over to balance between her knees, a fat hand reaching for the sweet. She popped the treat into his mouth.

I had gone to school with six of the Quiroz children, and I remembered the sight of Trinidad's rusted pickup, clanging and bouncing up to the school yard, the bed overflowing with laughing, squealing kids, his own and children picked up on the way. As long as their feet were dry and their shoes were clean of river mud, they could attend the El Polvo school. Each of Trinidad's children had finished the eighth grade, but while a handful of us went on to make the fifty-mile bus ride to high school in Presidio, the Quiroz children had gone to work full-time.

Florinda and I made polite conversation about the baby and passed on information about common acquaintances on either side. She poured a glass of tepid water from a blue glass pitcher on a table by the open door and handed it to me, a precious offering of hospitality since the family hauled all their water for cooking and drinking. Her mother came around from the kitchen, bringing with her the smell of fresh masa and the pungent aroma of chilies, and invited me to share the evening meal, careful to explain that Joe would welcome me were he not out with the goats. Cordelia brought up the subject of Trinidad's old friend and employer, clucking her tongue over the tragedy of Rhea's death. Florinda ducked her head and nuzzled the baby's thick hair.

"It's so sad for Grandfather," Florinda remarked. She looked surprised when I asked how they had gotten word of Rhea's death, then shrugged and said matter-of-factly, "Word passes. The Letter Man came with money from Abelardo, and also with the news."

I should have guessed the most likely source for passing along the news of Rhea's death would be Glafiro Paredes. The locals trusted him with cash-filled envelopes sent in care of El Polvo general delivery from Mexican nationals working in the U.S. to relatives in the closer Chihuahuan pueblos. More, they relished the news he brought, accepting with good grace the proselytizing that came with it. "He talks better than a priest," Trinidad had once said of the *predicador*.

"As soon as the Letter Man arrived, Grandfather asked about the *curandera*. He was worried about her, I think," Florinda said.

Cordelia glanced back into the interior of the house, then looked at me, leaning forward to whisper, "He's very sick with the sugar disease."

Florinda said, "The doctor at the clinic in Ojinaga says Grandfather must go into the hospital."

Cordelia said, "He saw the doctor six weeks ago. He has some pills, but he's still too sick to work."

That took care of one worry. If Trinidad had been sick at home for six weeks, he'd been safe from exposure to White Dog. It also explained why Trinidad had not been seen lately on the U.S. side. Though even if he'd been well, he might not have come forward after hearing the news that Rhea had been murdered. No one on this side, and not too many on the other, welcomed involvement with the authorities. Like many old border hands, Trinidad had never had a green card.

"I'm sorry to hear Trinidad has diabetes," I said. "Will he go to the hospital, do you think?"

"No," Florinda said. She glanced at her mother and got a nod in return. "Maybe you could talk to him, say it would be a good thing for him to do."

I promised to try. Cordelia stood up and said she'd take me to her father-in-law. We left Florinda playing with the baby on the rug.

Trinidad lay propped on a narrow cot, covered with a handwoven coverlet except for his bare feet, which he pushed outside the covers as we walked in. Cordelia chided him and tucked the coverlet in tightly around his feet. The old man protested that his feet were burning.

I was shocked at how ill he looked. The skin of his face, lined and brown as fine leather, had a flaccid appearance, as if the already tiny old man had lost pounds he never had. Even his voice, when he asked Cordelia if she had invited me to eat with them, sounded deflated and empty.

I assured him that both women had made me welcome. As I settled onto a stool by the bed, I heard Cordelia's tire-tread huaraches slapping against the floor as she crossed the main room on her way back to the kitchen shed.

For a few minutes I answered Trinidad's polite questions about my health, my husband, the trading post, but it seemed to me that he was already tired, so I came to the subject of my visit sooner than called for by courtesy.

As I mentioned Rhea Fair's name, I noticed Trinidad's callused hands clutch nervously as his faded eyes, the skin around them permanently creased from a lifetime of squinting against the sun's glare, stared up into mine.

"Señora Fair had much misfortune in her life, now in her death," he said. "I think a *bruja* caused the bad things that happened to her. Her husband killed by a falling horse, her baby daughter dying from snakebite, her sons smuggling drugs. Because of them, she lost her home." He fell back against the pillows and briefly closed his eyes, then continued, "She was healing me of this wasting illness. Now, I don't think I will live many weeks."

Knowing in my heart it would do no good, I nonetheless kept my promise to Cordelia. "The doctors at the hospital can make you feel better and get stronger."

Feebly he motioned his disagreement with a hand. "It's my time. Doctors can't save the spirit, many times not even the body. When my weakness got worse," he said, staring at the opposite wall where a crucifix hung, "Señora Fair told me, 'Go home, Trinidad, and let Cordelia take care of you. And at nine each morning and evening, I will think of your illness.'" Trinidad rolled his head in my direction and placed his hands on either side of his sunken stomach. "With my hands so," he said, "I thought of the healing. For many days I felt a warmth moving through me at these times. Always, afterward, I felt stronger. Then, seven days ago it stopped. I felt the healing that morning, but nothing since. I knew something was wrong. Then the Letter Man brought the news."

Trinidad's confidence in Rhea's ability as a *curandera* did not surprise me. Such faith in folk healing is common in the borderland. Folk healing is inexpensive and nonthreatening, practitioners abound, and the honest ones accept payment in simple gifts of food and clothing.

What astonished me was Trinidad's revelation that Rhea had practiced mental healing. Practitioners usually claimed to have the power to fix their minds at something they call an alpha level and heal the sick by thought, fixing the fee according to the magnitude of the brain wave, apparently. It rated right up there in my mind with a preacher I heard once who promised salvation for everyone who put fifty dollars or more in the collection plate. Healers of many faiths preyed on hope.

"She wasn't a fake," Trinidad said.

I flushed with embarrassment. "Reading my mind?"

"No. Your face. I know you think it's crazy, but she could heal. It wasn't something she wanted to do. It came to her."

"A gift from God," I said, quoting Charlie.

"Yes. That's just what she said. Some *remedios* she said she'd learned from her mother, and a *curandera* on this side taught her many things. She collected the herbs because, like me, she had no money for doctors."

"How did she discover she had this other power?" I asked.

"People on this side knew she learned healing from Guadalupe Paz, and when our *curandera* died, the people turned to Señora Fair. She was too kind to say no to them."

"I know many people went to her for help."

"Every week someone came, and others sent word. One time, this man came to get herbs for his wife, and when Señora Fair gave them to the husband she could see a hot spot, she called it, around his shoulder. As if the skin glowed through his shirt. She asked him what caused the pain in his shoulder. He told her he'd hurt it three years before in a fall, and since that time the pain had never left him. She placed her hands on his shoulder. She said she had a feeling of something flowing through both of them. When she took away her hands the man told her the pain had gone. He said he felt heat ripple through him as soon as she touched the shoulder. I know this man myself, and he has no more pain. Word spread and people came. It scared Señora Fair at first, I think. But she accustomed herself and accepted the gift. Later she learned that to think of the person's pain or sickness brought the healing without her presence."

The old man's voice had weakened to a raspy whisper. I sat quietly, giving him time to recover. Exhausted or not, he could not keep still, but restlessly moved his arms and legs, again kicking the blanket from his feet.

It slipped to the floor and I picked it up, folded it, and put it on one side of the bed. "Who killed her, Trinidad? You knew her better than anyone else."

"No, I knew her longer. From the time she came here and married Señor Jake. Your friend the schoolteacher could have told you about her. A very educated lady, Maria Deed. Señora Fair had great respect for her opinion. I drove her to see the schoolteacher for advice."

"When was this?"

"It was in the spring, early. I had to leave Joe to tend the kid goats alone while I drove her to the schoolhouse. She was worried about something and wanted to ask the schoolteacher for advice."

"About what, do you know?"

"Maybe something to do with the law. She carried some papers for the schoolteacher to look at."

I thought about that, but it could mean anything or nothing. Many locals had turned to Maria for help reading letters, filling out forms, writing letters, reading a map, or addressing a package. At the trading post, I got some of the same requests, though most often I was asked to help with long distance telephone calls. The *ejidos* had no electricity or water, let alone telephone service.

"She wasn't worried anymore," Trinidad was saying, "after she talked to the schoolteacher." The old man's forehead creased with the effort of remembering. "She said something about the newspaper. Something she read, maybe. The *fuerenos,* the outsiders from El Paso who came to see her, brought newspapers and old magazines. She liked to look at the pictures, and sometimes she read them. Then she would use them to start the fire."

I remembered the piles of dry, yellowing newspapers in the front room of Rhea's house next to the woodstove. But how could something she had read over six months ago touch on her murder?

"What about her sons?" I asked. "She kept in touch with them, I guess?"

"She sent money when she had any. None ever

came the other way,'' he answered, then broke into a fit of coughing.

I picked up a pitcher from the bedside table and started to pour what I thought was water. I stopped when I saw pale green liquid splash into the glass.

Trinidad nodded and reached for the glass. ''It's a tea made with begonia leaves. Good for my sickness. My son's wife grows the plants in the kitchen window.'' He handed the empty glass back to me and once more let his head collapse onto the pillow.

Out of the corner of my eye I saw Florinda edge her way to the door and peek in, a look of concern on her face. Time for me to leave. I stood up, but Trinidad spoke again, and I sat back down to let him finish.

''Señora Fair worried over letters. It would take her days to write one. But she did write one, a long one. More than one page. She wrote it right before I came home. She asked me to tell the Letter Man to come and get it for her.''

''Glafiro Paredes collected a letter from her?''

''I told him to, and he said he would. He's very faithful to his word.''

''Do you know whom she wrote to?''

He rolled his head from side to side on the pillow. I felt guilty. My questions had exhausted the old man. I leaned forward and patted his arm. ''I'll come for another visit soon.''

He squeezed my hand with dry, hot fingers. ''About her death...'' His voice quavered. ''Come back and tell me when they know exactly how she died.''

He said the words with such intensity that I promised I would, wondering why it mattered so much to him exactly how Rhea had died. Florinda waited for me at the doorway to show me out.

The evening still lingered as I started home. Behind me the sun went down in a glow of fiery red behind the hills of Mexico, while ahead the last long reach of light turned the tops of the Sierra Vieja range brilliant gold.

The dying light meant I had to watch carefully in order not to stray from the track, but this didn't prevent me from thinking about Rhea's death. Her growing fame as a *curandera* had brought strangers to her door. Had her killer been one among them who blamed Rhea for a failed cure and murdered her out of anger and anguish?

The sky had turned smoky blue. I cut on the headlights and the beams caught the reflected cold suns of a pair of eyes that blinked and vanished before I could identify the animal. As the earth cooled, the desert came to life, the silence of day replaced by a crescendo of grasshoppers, katydids, and crickets, and dominating all, the trill of a nighthawk hovering above, silhouetted against the afterlight.

On the desert floor the hunters and the hunted came out. Snakes, kangaroo rats, tarantulas, and owls scurried and scrambled, darted or glided from holes and burrows, warm-blooded and cold-blooded waiting patiently in ambush for each other.

Had Rhea's killer been as cold-blooded and casual as Andalon believed? Or had the murderer waited in ambush like a predator to take advantage of an opportune moment?

The remaining glow of light vanished, and the tips

of the mountains faded to black. Overhead, the Milky Way made a luminous smear across the starry sky. There are moments in such utter darkness, with the enveloping heavens so sharp in the clean air, when I almost feel the earth's spin, the galaxy's rush toward the edges of the expanding universe.

Pulling myself back from infinity, I crossed the river and steered carefully to the point where the bank leveled off to meet the empty road. There I turned right, toward home, following the tunnel of light cut by the headlights into the moonless dark.

The disruption in the darkness came at the first curve. I soon realized that what I thought were the few lights of El Polvo were too bright, too close, and on the wrong side of the road.

SEVEN

BILLY DEED'S white Nissan was parked at an angle on the riverbank, headlights on high beam aimed like twin spotlights at a cluster of salt cedars at the water's edge. I parked behind him. I could see a flashlight moving among the trees. A horse, its head drooping, stood nearby, the slack reins of the bridle tied to a limb. A pair of hounds rested at its feet.

I assumed there had been an accident. With the rough road and steep grade, about once a year some unlucky driver misses a curve and rolls his vehicle. Our last traffic fatality had been a twenty-nine-year-old man who lost control and spun off the road late one night. The next morning the UPS man spotted the overturned truck and found the man pinned in the wreckage. During the 139-mile trip to the nearest hospital, the injured man died from loss of blood. In the city, if you stop and gawk at an accident scene, you're a ghoul. Out here, given our lonely roads and long distances, stopping to render aid is an unwritten law.

"Anything I can do to help?" I called out as I started down, first-aid kit in hand.

The horse lifted its head, and Jerry Ayrs, a tall man in a thick long-sleeved shirt and chaps protecting his jeans, moved out from behind the animal. At the same time, I saw the flashlight turn in my direction, and Billy pushed out of the trees and walked toward me.

Maria's son is exceptionally handsome. He looks like a Spanish grandee sculpted in bronze, having inherited the blended Seminole-Black color of his father and the aquiline features of his maternal grandfather.

"Nothing anybody can do, Texana. Got an illegal, been dead for days," Billy said.

"You need me any longer?" Jerry asked.

"Nah," Billy said. "You can get on home. Sorry it took me so long to get here."

I had moved closer to meet Billy and, blinded by the headlights, I knew only by the squeak of the saddle leather that Jerry had mounted. As horse and rider moved up the bank and away, I heard Jerry's soft voice calling to the dogs, "Heeyah, heeyah."

"Glad you stopped," Billy said, and his relieved tone told me that he was glad not to be alone with a dead body here in the inky dark.

"Poor guy was wearing two pair of pants to protect him from snakebite," Billy said. "I guess a snake of one kind or the other musta got him. If it wasn't a rattler, it was a smuggler probably killed him. Illegals don't die of heatstroke this time of year. Jerry found him about six o'clock, but by the time he got to a phone it was seven. I was up at the Darke Ranch checking on a missing horse so I didn't get here until about five minutes ago. Good thing Jerry waited. I'd never have found the body looking on my own. What isn't scattered, is about melted into the ground."

The description reminded me of finding Rhea. Involuntarily, I shivered and gulped. Billy noticed, realized what he'd said, and quickly apologized for being too graphic. "Jerry will be late getting home," he remarked, changing the subject awkwardly but with good intention.

Home for Jerry is a house on the thirty-eight thousand acres he leases. When he's not tending the four hundred head of cattle he runs, he cowboys for the United States Department of Agriculture. An animal health technician, the agriculture department calls him. Jerry's job is to ride the river looking for Mexican cattle and horses that have waded across the Rio Grande, possibly bringing tick fever with them. Today's find had been a dead man.

The sound of a rough-running engine broke our silent isolation. "Can't be Dennis," Billy said, staring into the dark in the direction I had come from. I had been looking that way, too, trying to see headlights, but none were visible. As I turned back, I noticed Billy fingering the pistol at his hip. "We're edgy," I said. "There have been too many deaths."

Billy, I considered, had reason to be edgy. His parents had been murdered only a little farther along this road, and in daylight. With six thousand people in the county and three unexplained deaths in the past six months—four if we counted the man in the trees behind us—I considered the county probably had a higher murder rate than Dallas, maybe even New York.

The sound of the motor had been growing louder and louder. In open space, devoid of intervening noise and buildings that muffle or confuse sounds, a voice can carry for hundreds of yards, and a noisy pickup can be heard a mile or more in all directions.

"That's the Letter Man's pickup," Billy said. "I recognize the grind of the motor."

"And he's only got one headlight," I said, watching the weak beam that was so out of alignment it illuminated more of the roadside than the road. Billy and I stood at attention, intent upon what was coming like children watching for a parade. Finally the creeping vehicle arrived at a spot on the road above us and simply stopped, whether deliberately or from a breakdown it was impossible to judge.

From the cab, Glafiro Paredes's strong voice hailed us: *"¿Qué pasa?"*

Billy told him what was going on, and the old man got out and came down to join us, moving with agility. Glafiro has no birth certificate, no knowledge of the year of his birth, but guesses himself to be about seventy years old. He is thin and wiry, with bright eyes and a smile that shows both his golden heart and his gold-filled teeth.

"Is everything all right with you, señor?" Billy asked. "You're running late."

"Oh, yes," Glafiro said agreeably. "My pickup suffered a breakdown this afternoon, but I patched her together and here we are. I will have to write to my brothers in the mission church at Presidio and ask if they will send some parts for repair."

"I keep plenty of auto parts in stock," I said. "What do you need?"

The dignified old man sighed and answered, "Almost everything, I fear." He counted on his fingers: "Spark plugs, water pump, belts, carburetor." He shook his head. "Alas, too much." He looked around us toward the trees and nodded in that direction. "This poor dead man, is he known to us?"

"No way of telling," Billy said. "No identification. A few pesos in one pocket and a broken compass in the other."

"One of us, then," Glafiro said, meaning a Mexican national. When he isn't delivering the mail and preaching, Glafiro lives in a lean-to shed across the river from El Polvo.

From the southeast, bright lights swept down the road, and another pickup stopped. A door slammed and the bulky figure of Dennis Bustamente bounded toward us, a plastic bag in his hand. The deputy acknowledged the Letter Man and me with a nod and a grim smile, accepting our presence at the scene as unremarkable, and turned to Billy to ask about the dead man. I had no desire to remain for the grisly cleanup work, so I offered to follow Glafiro home, in case of another breakdown. He accepted, took my arm to help me up the bank, and escorted me to my pickup.

"You lead, and I shall follow," he told me.

I warned him, "Honk if I go too fast."

"The horn does not work either," he replied, shutting my door.

Only occasionally did I let the needle move past thirty on the speedometer, and I kept a watchful eye on the rearview mirror to make sure the single, baleful headlight still followed. Once it dropped back and I slowed to twenty-five, then twenty. At ten miles per hour the headlight suddenly surged toward my bumper. After that, Glafiro managed to stay close and maintain a steady speed. We arrived at El Polvo twenty minutes later. At the edge of town where the scattering of trailers sits, I stopped to wave him on. Fording the river here is easy and Glafiro's shed is only a few hundred feet on the other side.

Glafiro had turned the pickup toward the river when I honked. He stopped, reversed, seemed to experience difficulty with the steering, and finally just stopped. I drove up beside his pickup, but before I could get out, he was at my door. I cut on the dome light so we could see each other.

"I remembered something I wanted to ask you," I explained.

He bowed his head slightly and smiled.

I chewed my lip, a bad habit of mine when I'm ill at ease or embarrassed. I didn't know how to ask what I wanted to know without seeming to imply a certain nosiness on Glafiro's part about the mail he delivered, and the last thing I wanted was to offend him.

"I saw Trinidad today," I said, beginning at the beginning.

"How is his health?"

"Not very good."

"I'm sorry to hear this news." He smiled up at me patiently, seemingly willing to wait forever for me to come to the point of why I was keeping him from his bed and sleep.

"He mentioned that Mrs. Fair had entrusted a letter to you."

"She did. Joe asked me to pick it up and mail it for her, and I did so."

"When was this?"

He thought about it, frowning slightly. "When Trinidad learned the news of his illness. I do not know the date, but it was over a month ago. If the date is important, it will be recorded at the clinic."

"What may be important is the name of the person Rhea Fair wrote to. Do you recall the name or address?"

He looked down, absently scratching at an inflamed cut on his hand. "The address I do not know. The name made me laugh. Anglo names are so odd. This one was a Spanish word, *fonda*. Like a market stall. That's what *fondas* are."

"And the first name?"

He shook his head. "It was short, I think, and awkward to sound, but no, I can't remember it."

I thanked him and let him go on his way. I heard his door slam, and I had backed up and started to turn when Glafiro's voice floated out of the darkness from the far side of the river.

"There was an answering letter," he said. "It came general delivery. I took it to Señora Fair maybe the week before last, I think."

"*Gracias,*" I called to him. I watched the taillights of his pickup, both working, vanish into the trees before I headed for home.

This time Clay had arrived home first. His pickup was in place next to Charlie's Cadillac. I was happy to see that Charlie's visit wasn't over. Usually his stops are as unpredictable as they are short. Five days is the longest he has ever stayed with us. This time of year, with the fall tourist season peaked and closing at the end of the month, Charlie's help in inventory and restocking comes in handy. If he doesn't

leave tomorrow, I thought, I'll ask him to stay while
I make the 325-mile trip to El Paso to stock up on
clothes and housewares for resale.

As soon as I shut the kitchen door I saw the note.
Clay had left it propped against a glass on the counter
by the nightlight. I picked it up and held it closer to
the light and farther from my eyes—I refuse to admit
I need reading glasses.

*Andalon says the woman in the white Suburban
is Linden Fonda, from San Antonio. Reported
missing by her aunt Nov. 1. Don't call him tonight. He said he wants to get some sleep.*

EIGHT

CLAY LADLED scrambled eggs onto our plates and in answer to my unasked question said, "Andalon didn't elaborate."

I stood in the doorway, groggy with sleep but becoming more alert with every sniff of the scent of coffee steaming from the pot. I had spent a restless night battling bad dreams about finding Rhea's body, though in my nightmare Rhea's body had Maria's face. I was never more grateful that Clay customarily cooked breakfast.

I poured the coffee and set the cups and the coffeepot on the table, pulled out my chair, and let my husband serve me. The puffy, golden mounds of eggs were wonderfully fragrant because of their freshness. We get a half dozen now and then delivered by a neighbor from downriver. He keeps the chickens in a coop, but in spite of the fencing the foxes and coyotes manage to dig under, so he is constantly having to replace the hens. Plus the stress puts the survivors off their laying.

"There's one bit of news," Clay said, putting the plate of toast between us and sitting down at the table. "The flag's flying at the Darke Ranch."

"So Robert is in residence, is he. When did you find this out?"

"Lank left a message on the machine last night. Wants me to check over a horse with a cut on its leg. Lank already did the stitching. He's more than competent, but Robert insisted on having me check the animal.''

"Billy mentioned something about a horse last night, but I thought he said it had been stolen or was missing.''

"Probably the same one. Got out of the pasture where they keep the saddle horses and came back hurt.''

"If Robert's back, can fiesta be far behind? What would we do for the social season without the annual Darke soiree,'' I said in pleasurable anticipation.

The Darke fall fiesta, we locals call it, when Robert entertains upward of 150 guests flown in to hunt, dine, and dance at his considerable expense. On the day before the party, private planes land and take off almost nonstop at the airstrip above the house, and several acres of one of the lower pastures become a parking lot for Suburbans. The day is a double boon for the community. Robert hires locals as extra guides to conduct hunts, as drivers to chauffeur guests and luggage between airstrip and house, and to clean, cook, and serve. The second boon comes in an open invitation to the dinner and dance. I like Robert's diplomacy and democracy in inviting the community, but Clay has rather resented Robert's parties ever since he overheard one of the urbanite guests, staring at a group of us, remark: "Aren't they perfect! Clones from a Clint Eastwood Western.''

"Once you get there and get some of that great food and drink into you, you'll enjoy yourself,'' I told him, already thinking about what I would wear.

"Uhm,'' he said, but his attention remained focused on the papers he had propped against the creamer. The document was the current report from the Zoonosis Control Division of the Bureau of Veterinary Public Health summarizing rabies activity for the month. He had read it often enough to have it memorized. The concentration was a sign that he anticipated the worst from the brain tissue tests on the coyote and White Dog. When Clay worries about something, he focuses on it relentlessly, taking solace, I suppose, in facts. I gave up on conversation, turning my eyes to the day-old Presidio *International* by my plate, but thinking more about what I wanted to ask Andalon than the headlines in the newspaper.

We ate our toast and eggs in silent anxiety. Clay finished first, and I poured myself one last cup of coffee. The loud bell of the telephone, ringing through from the line at his office, startled us both.

Clay lifted the receiver and answered, "The vet." A pause. "I'm clear this morning. If you can get the cattle in, I'll be there by eight."

I carried my empty cup to the sink and started the washing-up.

He hung up and said, "Well, it's started. While Gwen Masters was putting out feed she saw a coyote attack one of her cows. Imagine if she hadn't seen the attack. In a couple of weeks, she might have gone out to feed the livestock and been mauled and possibly killed by a normally docile cow."

I asked the pertinent question: "Is her stock vaccinated?" If not, Clay would be gone all morning on the one call.

"Yes, thankfully. I'll revaccinate the bitten animal and let Gwen quarantine it there."

"Will you be back for lunch, do you think?"

"Probably, but don't count on it. If I have time, I'll swing by the Darke Ranch this morning."

"You'll be late, then. You and Robert never have short conversations," I said to his back as he went out the door. Moments later I heard his truck start and drive up the road. I switched on the answering machine to take his other calls, finished the dishes, and went through to the front counter and the business of the day.

Charlie had stayed and had busied himself sweeping off the front porch and dusting the tin folding chairs emblazoned with the Corona beer logo.

The morning ran as usual. I sold a bottle of aspirin and some candy to a woman and her three children from the other side. A rancher came in for a case of motor oil, and a couple of locals came in and paid their grocery bill. Charlie noticed the tin of the porch roof had come loose at one corner and we hauled out the ladder, which he held for me while I nailed the sheet back in place.

About 8:30 a.m. I bought a goat I didn't need from an old man in a pickup with more dings and dents than paint and without a windshield. He pulled up out front, the kid goat squirming, legs tired and hooves drumming against the steel of the pickup bed. A young Mexican, legs dangling over the collapsed tailgate, steadied the frightened animal with one hand.

"Es un cabrito," the man said.

We haggled for a bit before agreeing on a price, and I had the man unload the goat into one of Clay's pens in back. I paid him in cash, and he promptly spent it on cigarettes and *cerveza*. It wasn't until he drove off that I noticed that the young Mexican had stayed behind. He stood, uncertain and nervous, in the shade around the corner of the porch until I smiled encouragingly, and he stepped forward.

He wore tennis shoes, polyester pants, and a brown knit shirt already stained with sweat, more from nerves than exertion, I imagined. He had probably spent an exhausting night on the other side, waiting for daylight to know where he was, then paying the old man in the pickup a few pesos to bring him across. He followed me inside and walked the aisles fingering this and that. He looked both honest and scared, but I kept my eyes on him and my hand near the loaded pistol on a shelf beneath the cash register. He selected a number of items and brought them to the counter. I rang up three cans of sardines, a loaf of bread, and six candy bars. He paid in pesos. I started to sack his purchases, but he shook his head and put them into the string bag tied to his waist. I told him he could refill his water jug at the faucet out back.

He almost left then, turning halfway to go, then looking back at me from under a thatch of black hair so thick it stood in tufts. I guessed his age at seventeen or eighteen. He reached into the pocket of his pants and brought out a small square of paper, which he unfolded with great care, placed on the counter, and smoothed out with his hand. He pointed to it and said, "Please, where?"

That he asked the question at all indicated a desperate need to know. Intrigued, I looked at the paper, a page torn from a magazine, the creases worn white and thin from having been folded and unfolded many times. It was a color photograph taken at night of the skyline of a city, the buildings outlined with Christmas lights. Most of the caption was missing except for the name of the city: Dallas.

I sighed and led him over to the far wall where most of the space is taken up by framed maps of the county, state, and the U.S. I pointed to a dot on the state map that represents El Polvo, then traced my finger along the route of the six-hundred-odd miles to Dallas.

The young man nodded as if he understood.

"It's a long way," I cautioned him.

He shrugged. *"Ni modo,"* he said, an expressive phrase implying he had little choice, since there was nothing for him in his country.

He turned his gaze back to the map, but the baffled look on his face told me it was the first map he had ever seen. His grasp of the U.S. was a direction, *el norte,* and an image formed from magazines, movies, and tales of those who had crossed over. The lucky Mexicans had help getting across from older brothers or friends who knew the unmarked routes through the maze of scrub, fence lines, *senderos,* and ranch roads. The journey required stamina and the good fortune not to run out of food or water or get lost and walk in circles. Others, those who could borrow or save enough, paid a fixer to arrange a crossing to an agreed-upon destination on this side. Too often these chickens, as they are called by the "coyotes" who transport them, are robbed, sometimes killed, by those paid to help them.

The young man gave the map a long, puzzled look.

I tried showing him on the county map our present location. He thanked me gravely and turned to go. I told him to wait, stepped behind the counter and removed a state road map from the display rack, picked up a pen, and marked the route. I handed it to him along with a cheap pocket compass from a box beneath the counter.

He protested that he could not pay, and I pressed both into his hand and told him it was a gift. "For the sake of your mother."

I took him out back and showed him where to fill his water jug. Afterward, I watched him walk into the desert until his figure shrank to a dot on the horizon. I thought of the body found last night. That man, too, might have had a dream folded in his pocket.

Thirty minutes later I was back staring at the county map and wondering why I had not realized the implication earlier. The place where the man's body had been found was almost exactly opposite the beginning of the track that went past Rhea's place and on to the Darke Ranch. Billy had assumed the man had just crossed from the other side and then died. But what if he had been going back down the track before he died? He might have killed Rhea and died on the way back to Mexico. Unlike most of us, Rhea had not kept a gun, even for killing snakes. She'd always boasted that White Dog killed any rattler he saw. But she could have fought the man, struck him with something, perhaps. Or he might have been injured or killed by someone else. I thought of the oblong space of flattened grass near Rhea's house, dotted with drops of blood. Had the

man collapsed there, recovered his strength, and
made his way to the river, where he died? Or a third
person might have killed them both, the man simply
taking longer to die, trying to go home. I badly
wanted to talk to Andalon.

I dialed the sheriff's office, but the deputy on duty
said the sheriff was out. With four men in the department to cover almost four thousand square miles,
Andalon is seldom in.

For lunch, I prepared four steak sandwiches and
microwaved frozen hash brown potatoes, then called
Charlie. He ate two of the sandwiches and three help-
ings of potatoes. At one in the afternoon, with Clay
not yet back, I left Charlie in charge and drove over
to the post office to collect the mail and ask Lucy
Ramos if she could tell me anything about Rhea's
mail.

Ever since I can remember, Everett Barron has
been making the 111-mile drive from Marfa to El
Polvo to bring the mail. He also brings our dry cleaning, prescription drugs, and sometimes milk and ba-
con. His postal van was parked in front of Lucy's
adobe when I got there. On my way in, I stopped to
pat Lucy's dog, a gigantic and mellow old mutt who
spent most of his time as he was now, dozing on the
tattered couch that years ago had been brought outside and had served since as an upholstered bench
by the front door. Couch and dog are always in the
shade. When Lucy had first married, she had her husband dig up cottonwood saplings from the river and
plant them along the road in front of the adobe. For
years a succession of Lucy's sons hauled water from
the river for the thirsty trees. Then the taproots hit

the water table and the trees shot up. There is no more soothing sound in the world than the papery rustle of the leaves of the cottonwood trees that shade Lucy's home.

Inside the tiny front room that is the post office, Lucy was putting letters into the wooden postal boxes while chattering to Everett about her grandson's new partnership in a law office in San Antonio.

Everett, loaded down with outgoing mail, greeted me, and Lucy, peering over her shoulder, announced, "No mail for you today, Texana."

Everett left, and I waited until Lucy finished sorting the last pile of letters before asking her about Rhea Fair's mail.

"Oh, I remember those letters," Lucy said, "because the *curandera* never sent or wrote letters."

"Do you recall the day Rhea mailed the letter to this Linden Fonda in San Antonio?"

"No, but I do know when the letter came for Rhea because it was the birthday of Mario, the youngest son of my nephew Jorge, and we had the party here. That morning, Glafiro's pickup broke down and stayed out front all night. My nephew came the next day and fixed whatever was broken, but he told Glafiro to take the pickup in to a *carroceria* and have it worked on properly. That Glafiro, all he could think about was getting that letter to the *curandera*. He said Señora Fair's letter must be very important because it was the only one he ever remembered her getting."

"And the day?"

Lucy took down the wall calendar and turned it back to the previous month, tilting her head back to look through the bottom half of her bifocals. She stabbed a finger at a circled date. "October 21. A Friday."

I thanked Lucy and left. I was getting into my pickup when Lucy's head popped out the doorway and she shouted, "Doña Aurora wants to see you." I waved and nodded, acknowledging Lucy's instructions. Doña Aurora is a clairvoyant whose particular skill is in finding lost objects and telling fortunes. She is known as the godmother of El Polvo because it is considered good luck to have her stand as godmother at a christening. I couldn't imagine why she wanted to see me, but I'd find out soon enough. Her adobe is on the ridge above the cemetery, not three hundred yards away.

As I drove, I pondered what, if anything, I had learned. Six weeks ago, Rhea had written a letter to Linden Fonda in San Antonio. On the twenty-first of October, she had received an answer. On the twenty-fourth, Eliot Lofts had picked up some herbal tea from her, and her son Matt had been there. On the twenty-fifth, Trinidad claimed to have felt Rhea's healing power for the last time. On the first of November, I found her body.

What, if anything, did the letter have to do with her death? And what had happened to Linden Fonda? Aurora Cortes is a clairvoyant. Maybe she could tell me.

I parked between the wall of the cemetery and the stone steps up to the small, square house.

The front door stood open and Doña Aurora waited there, leaning on her walker, a tiny woman with shining benevolent eyes and thin silver hair pulled back in a tight bun.

"Pour that water on my geraniums, please, and come inside," she instructed me.

A tiny bucket, half filled with water, stood by the steps. I lifted it and splashed water into each of the six blooming plants growing in coffee cans painted red and spaced along the top of the low wall that surrounds the tiny front patio. I set the empty bucket back where I found it.

Doña Aurora's front door is wood, painted a bright blue. It opens directly into the front room. She was seated on the edge of a brass bed that took up most of one wall. The only other furniture was a vintage 1930s chrome and red-laminated table. On the wall above the table hangs a gilt-framed picture of the Virgin of Guadalupe. Prayer candles covered the surface of the table, along with plaster statues of Doña Aurora's favorite saints. I recognized St. Martin, the black saint of Peru noted for healing and feeding both needy humans and animals, St. Antony, patron saint of the poor and of lost objects, and Doña Aurora's personal favorite, Jude, saint of lost causes. The wall above her bed was covered with row after row of framed photographs of children, each a godchild.

"There are three generations of families on that wall," she said. "I was as young as some of those children when I learned I had the power to know things about people's lives. I thought it was a game. One day, the cousin of my mother came to our house complaining that someone had stolen fourteen thousand pesos, all the money he had in the world, from where he had hidden it in his house. A name came into my head and without thinking I spoke: 'Octavio took the money.' Straight away, my mother's cousin went to confront his friend. The man, believing he must have been seen, admitted taking the money. They fought, and my mother's cousin stabbed Octavio and killed him. From this time, I understood that the power to see could be dangerous. One must not be an instrument of evil.''

I knew what she alluded to. Many clairvoyants and healers practiced witchcraft, selling hexes guaranteed to bring love, harm an enemy, secure riches. There are people on both sides of the river who are truly spooked by the fear of witches and have no doubt that a witch can put a spell on someone. When I was a child, a man from across the river shot a neighbor because he believed the woman had put a hex on his wife, making her ill. And within the past year, the newspapers had carried a story about a woman in the lower Rio Grande valley who had hired a *curandera* to put a death hex on the young man who had jilted the woman's daughter. The *curandera,* to ensure the spell worked, had her husband murder the young man. Even Maria had admitted to me that, when in high school, she had paid a *curandera* in Ojinaga to put a hex on a boy from Marfa to make him like her. "It didn't work," Maria had said, embarrassed at having told me. Anyone with Doña Aurora's power as a seer had to be cautious. People hate and fear witches, and such feelings can spread as fast as rumor.

"To work for evil intent is to soil one's soul," Doña Aurora was saying.

I listened and said nothing. Doña Aurora read my palm when I was sixteen. Maria and I had come together, giggling and nervous, to have our fortunes told. For Maria, the seer had predicted a marriage to a dark man, a union that would displease her father but make Maria happy. Doña Aurora had been old even then, but her eyes had intelligence and certitude in them when she looked up from reading my palm to tell me that I would have a bad emotional experience in marriage, but that a second relationship would be happy—this four years before I met the man who would become my first husband. How could she have known? "Spooky," I told Maria after my divorce.

Doña Aurora gestured toward the table. "The cards, my reading the palm, these are tools. People feel the need to see that my knowledge comes from somewhere, from the cards or from something written in their palm. But what I see is not there. Unbidden, the thoughts come into my head. Like the name *Octavio*. Or that someone's missing keys are in a jar on a kitchen shelf."

She looked hesitant, as if whatever she had to tell me next worried her. I waited, watching her face, giving her time to say something else.

"In the spring, Rhea Fair came to me for help. She believed someone had put an evil eye on her."

I cleared my throat and tried to imagine the seriousness of the evil eye to Rhea. Believers attributed sickness and even death to such a thing. It gave a meaning, something to blame, for the failures, illnesses, and miseries of life. A kind of closure, I suppose.

Doña Aurora said, "For many years I have limited myself to seeing the future." She shifted her gnarled hands on the walker, pulled herself upright, and tugged her sweater tighter around her stooped shoulders. "As a young woman, I practiced as a *curandera*. Rhea knew of this and asked me to give her a ritual cleansing to counteract the evil eye. I used the egg of a turkey for the sweeping, because of the yolk's special power to absorb evil."

The ritual cleansing that Doña Aurora spoke of restored harmony and energy to the body. The *curandera*, while reciting certain prayers such as the Apostles' Creed, moved the egg in a sweeping motion over the victim's body. Afterward the egg would be burned so the victim could see the evil destroyed and know he could no longer be harmed. For the sweeping to work, faith is necessary. Faith, Maria had remarked, is the first step to understanding. I must admit, I don't have too much faith.

With infinite slowness and dignity Doña Aurora pushed her walker before her, drawing herself after it, moving toward the table. I followed, ready to steady her, but she did not need me. Reaching the table, she paused, released one hand from its hold on the walker, and gripped my shoulder. She looked at me, and I saw her normal expression dissolve, become masklike. Her eyes looked blind.

"What's wrong?" I asked. "What are you seeing?"

As suddenly as her face had changed, it shifted back to normal. She didn't answer my questions but picked up a packet and a brown glass bottle from the table. She held them out to me. "Take these," she said, pushing them into my hands. "The little bottle contains a special herbal water. It must be sprayed in every corner of the trading post. The plastic bag contains incense, crushed leaves of herbs, and the seed of mustard. Sprinkle some inside the trading post and on the roof. The remainder keep on your person. It will protect you."

She dipped the tip of one finger into a greenish-gold liquid in a glass jar. "Bend your head to me."

I did as I was told and felt her cool fingertip touch my forehead and make the sign of the cross. As she did, I smelled a slightly resinous odor.

She placed her hands on top of my head.

"All-powerful and all-wise God, protect this woman, I beg you, from all dangers, present and in the future…"

As Doña Aurora prayed, I closed my eyes and experienced that sudden physical wave of feeling one sometimes has in church at a particularly majestic or moving moment, for me, usually in the Easter or Christmas rituals, the rare occasions that I attend. I felt warmed by Doña Aurora's goodwill but lost as to why she thought I needed her blessing.

The slight weight of her hands lifted from my head. I opened my eyes.

The seer looked up at me, her eyes searching my face, for what I didn't know.

"My gift," she said, "is inherited. My father had it, and one of my daughters, though it frightens her. I do not invent things. I speak what I know as it comes to me."

"When I was sixteen, you told me my future held a bad marriage, then a good one."

"Did I? I seldom remember my predictions. The thought comes. I speak it, and it drops from my mind. I do not think I could bear the burden of full remembrance."

"You were correct in what you told me then. I don't doubt you."

She nodded her head and looked as if my answer pleased her. Then her face grew somber.

"There will be another death," she said emphatically. "Take care to protect yourself."

I swallowed. "Can you see anything else?"

She shook her head, lifted her walker, and turned away, moving toward the bed.

At that moment, if Doña Aurora had been wrong in her prediction about my marriages, I would have been happier.

NINE

THIS TIME when I telephoned the sheriff's office, Andalon answered. "Wait a minute until I find the report," he said. I could hear papers being shuffled on his desk.

"On the twenty-fifth of October, Linden Fonda booked an early-bird flight from San Antonio to Dallas to connect with Lone Star Airlines' 9:45 a.m. flight to Alpine. It gets in at 12:05 p.m. About 12:30, she picked up the Suburban she'd arranged to rent. We know she got to your place in it, and we assume she got to Mrs. Fair's, since the groceries she bought from you were there. The Suburban hasn't been returned. No word from Fonda to the rental agency. And before you ask, no one's reported an accident involving someone fitting the woman's description, and no one's seen the vehicle."

"It has to be somewhere," I said.

"I've put the border patrol on notice to keep an eye out."

I kept quiet, waiting for Andalon to fill me in on the rest.

"According to the San Antonio cop I talked to, Fonda's aunt reported her niece missing when Fonda failed to turn up at the hospital like she'd promised. Seems the aunt had surgery and Fonda said she'd be there to help with the checkout and to drive her aunt home."

"Does she live with this aunt?"

I could hear a page being turned. "No. Lives alone in an apartment."

"What about her parents?"

"Dead."

"What did the police find out?" I asked.

"Nothing. They checked out the apartment. No sign of any disturbance. TV and other valuables in plain sight. Fonda is a reporter for the *Express-News*. Been there three years. She requested a week of vacation beginning the twenty-fourth of October. She was due back at work the thirty-first of October. Didn't show. Hasn't been in touch."

I heard a truck stop out front and turned to look through the windows. I was using the telephone at the counter, rather than our house line. The double doors swung open and Charlie walked in carrying four grocery bags overflowing with sandwich loaves and hot dog and hamburger buns. I had taken advantage of his stay to send him into Presidio for bread. We are too far out and don't sell enough to have delivery.

"So what are the police doing?" I asked Andalon.

"Not wasting their time. Fonda's an adult. Until I called about her, they figured she was off somewhere with a boyfriend."

"And now?"

"Now it's our worry," Andalon said. "And there's not much we can do except keep our eyes open."

His attitude irritated me. "You're assuming she's dead, aren't you?"

"I hope she's with her boyfriend, like the San Antonio cops think. What I think is she could have visited Mrs. Fair, then gone on up the track through the Darke Ranch to Highway 90, and from there straight in to El Paso.''

''She'd have to know the way to follow that track without getting lost,'' I said.

''Unless she'd been that way before. Or someone drew her a map,'' he added.

''If a smuggler killed her, that Suburban could be in Chicago by now,'' I said.

''Now you're thinking like a sheriff.''

''And while I'm thinking like you, what about the grass with what looked like blood spots on it? Did you have it tested?''

''It's blood. That's the easy part.''

''If it's blood, could it be from the dead illegal?''

''That's stretching for a connection, don't you think?''

I didn't, but I bit my tongue to keep from saying so.

''Blood tests to show a match like that cost more than I'd care to authorize without more information about how he died. If it's murder, and if there's anything to show he's connected to Rhea Fair, then I'll spend the taxpayers' money. There's just one thing I can tell you,'' Andalon added. ''I haven't got the written autopsy report on Mrs. Fair, but I called the lab. I know how she died. Mrs. Fair was shot. Close-up. The killer stood in front of her and shot her through the eye.''

I gasped and sagged against the counter. That detail, coupled with my memory of her face, made me feel faint.

"Sorry if I upset you. I thought you wanted to know," Andalon said.

"No, it's okay." My words came out in a squeaky whisper that made Charlie turn around and look at me. I took a deep breath and tried again. "It's okay." I sounded better.

"She'd been dead about a week from the day you found her," he added.

Killed in the afternoon, I thought. Before dark, anyway. You'd need daylight to see to take aim. I managed to thank Andalon for calling and to say good-bye. But my mind was on Trinidad. Seven days before my visit to him, Trinidad had a feeling that something had happened to Rhea Fair because he no longer experienced the presence of her healing power. Seven days. Six days later, I had found Rhea's body. I checked the old-fashioned wall calendar I had bought in support of the volunteer fire department in Presidio. Trinidad's feeling corresponded with Andalon's fact: Rhea Fair had died on the twenty-fifth of October.

Shortly after my conversation with Andalon ended, I heard the back door bang and Clay came in whistling, stuck his head around the door, and shouted, "Great news!"

"The rabies tests are negative?" I said. His face fell, and I felt guilty for guessing incorrectly and breaking his mood.

"Not that good," he said. "No word from the lab yet." He smiled again. "But nearly as good. Robert Darke has volunteered to pick up the cost of rabies vaccine for local livestock and pets and as many strays as we can round up. And he's offered the help of his ranch hands.''

I raised my eyebrows. "You must have done wonders with that horse he wanted you to look at,'' I said.

"Oh, the horse is fine. Lank stitched him up okay. Nothing for me to do.''

"I know Robert is rich, and often generous. But somehow this doesn't seem like him. I wouldn't have called him philanthropic. His money usually goes to zany projects, or at least the kind with no immediate impact or results. What's his motive?''

Clay grinned. "Isn't it obvious?''

I thought about it. "The fiesta.''

"Exactly. He doesn't want his guests worried by a rabies scare. This doesn't eliminate the problem, of course, but it helps reduce the local danger from the disease while making Robert feel he's protecting his visitors.''

"When will you start?'' I asked, thinking about the logistics involved. Getting people to vaccinate their livestock and the half-wild cats and dogs that qualified as pets around here would be a feat.

Clay explained that he had ordered the vaccine by telephone while at the Darke Ranch and that he and Lank had mapped out a notification campaign. They divided the area up into quadrants and planned a telephone campaign to notify people about the vaccination drive. The ranch hands would personally get in touch with those without telephones, offering to take animals in to Clay's office. For anyone not willing, Clay would take the vaccine to the animal. The plan served two purposes: It would alert everyone of the rabies threat, and it would improve the vaccination rate for livestock and pets. Clay added that the roundup of strays would be catch as catch can, whenever the opportunity presented itself. Robert Darke had even agreed to supply extra cages for observation of suspect animals, plus dozens of humane traps.

"I can help," Charlie said.

"Great," Clay said. "The more the better. I'll put you in charge of a quadrant." He put a hand on my shoulder. "Any lunch left?"

"I'm surprised Robert didn't feed you."

"He offered. I didn't want to take the time. Too much organizing to do."

I left Charlie behind the counter and went to the kitchen, took the wrapped sandwich out of the refrigerator, and poured two glasses of iced tea. I sat at the table with Clay and sipped tea while he ate and talked some more about organizing the vaccination drive. When he had wound down, I told him what I'd learned from Andalon about Rhea's death and about Linden Fonda, including the letters that had passed between the two.

"So," he offered, "she could have murdered Rhea."

"Is that likely?"

"Why not." He shrugged. "She was there. You found the groceries she left. The timing's pretty close. This Fonda kid gets here on the twenty-fifth, right after, Rhea's dead."

"It's a possibility," I conceded. "I just think somehow, all this seems tied in with Rhea's being a *curandera.*"

He frowned. "But that's why the girl went to see her, isn't it?"

"I had that impression the day she bought the gas and groceries, but maybe I assumed too much. She could have been seeing Rhea for some other reason."

Clay finished the last bite of sandwich and helped himself to dessert from the cookie jar. I was thinking about Trinidad's comment that last spring Rhea had been so worried about something she had him drive her to the schoolhouse to get advice from Maria Deed. Trinidad believed the problem had to do with the law, but that was because Rhea had taken some papers with her. Legal papers, Trinidad had thought. Why? Possibly because to him any printed material meant momentous events: marriage, birth, death, and green cards.

That reminded me, and I said, "I promised Trinidad that I'd let him know how Rhea died. He seemed so anxious, I think I'll go see him this evening."

Clay brushed cookie crumbs from his shirtfront and said, "Let's go now. While you talk to Trinidad, I'll talk to Joe about helping get the word out on the other side about the free vaccinations. Won't do much good over here if we don't get the animals in at least the closest *ejidos* and pueblos."

In the sunlight of evening, the Rio Grande ran lavender-blue as we crossed into Mexico. I relaxed while Clay drove. We made no conversation, content in each other's company, secure with each other's silence.

However companionable our silence, I broke it. As we bumped over the collapsing rim of a hillock, something jogged my memory. "Put Jesse Waites on your list of folks with animals that need vaccinating."

Clay looked over at me. "I've never known Jesse to keep any livestock."

"Well, he's keeping some now. Why else did he buy needles and antibiotic?"

"What kind of antibiotic?"

"Some penicillin," I said.

Clay popped his hands against the steering wheel and laughed. "The old scudder's probably using it to doctor himself."

I stared at him. "My God, is it safe?"

"I don't recommend it, but lots of the old ranchers do it. Mostly they get away with it. I did know one who injected himself with enough to cure ten cows. He had an allergic reaction and had to be hospitalized for a rash and swelling."

"But you'll check on Jesse in case," I said.

"I think the only company Jesse wants or needs is his whiskey bottle and his old rifle. Lank tells me Jesse's taken to shooting at anything that moves up that canyon."

"I don't like the sound of that."

Clay looked over at me. "Don't worry," he said. "We'll find out if he's tamed a bobcat for company, but very carefully."

As we neared Trinidad's adobe, we caught up to a large herd of goats. Joe Quiroz was following the crush of animals while two spotted dogs circled at the edges of the herd. The tightly packed goats, accustomed to the routine, paid little attention to the yips and nips of the dogs.

Clay stopped the pickup and got out. "I'll walk in with Joe," he said.

I slid behind the wheel and drove on to the house. Cordelia met me at the yard gate. She had such a long, sad look on her face that I feared for Trinidad. Her first words seemed to confirm my fear.

"Welcome, Texana. A guest will help take our minds from our grief," she told me as she took my hand and drew me inside.

"Trinidad?"

She shook her head. "My husband's father is the same. Our sadness is for our son Hector. We have received word that he serves a sentence in a Texas jail, because too many times he has been arrested for being an illegal."

"I'm sorry," I told her, feeling helpless. Hector is the oldest son of the family. They depended on the money he sent home to clothe and feed the younger children and grandchildren.

"Come," Cordelia said, straightening her shoulders. "My husband's father has been fretting. I don't know what about. Perhaps you bring him news that will ease his mind."

She ushered me into Trinidad's room. If possible, he looked thinner and more frail than he had the day before. His black eyes seemed sunken and he acknowledged my presence with only the lifting of a thin hand on the blanket.

I sat down and Cordelia left us. Trinidad spoke as soon as she disappeared through the door.

"You have learned how Señora Fair died?"

I nodded, not at all certain whether I should tell him. But I had promised. And the dying, as Trinidad surely was unless he received a doctor's care, have as much right to know the truth as anyone. Perhaps more.

"Andalon told me her death came quickly. Too fast for her to have suffered," I said, trying to ease my way in. I had heard others use such words and thought them silly. How did we know that, simply because death happened in seconds, there was no suffering? Might not the pain, both physical and psychic, be equal to the moment? How many seconds of time are needed in order to experience fear, regret, despair?

Trinidad clutched at my arm. "How?" he rasped. Out of the corner of my eye, I saw Florinda standing in the doorway, anxious eyes on her grandfather.

"The killer shot her," I said.

Trinidad's eyes bored into mine. I felt compelled to add, "In the face. Through the eye."

The old man's mouth sagged open, and his eyes rolled.

I jumped up, thinking he had fainted, and tried to raise him up on the pillow. As I lifted his shoulders, his eyes refocused.

He said, "That's how you kill a witch."

"You kill a witch," he repeated as if he thought me uncomprehending, "by shooting it through the eye." He covered his face with his arms.

I stood there stunned, then felt a hand on my arm. Florinda pulled me away and guided me out of the bedroom.

"I'm sorry," I said.

"Don't be upset," she said.

She moved us farther out of earshot of her grandfather and explained, "That's an idea Grandfather has in his mind. When he was very young, he worked in the mines. It was a good job. Another man wanted Grandfather's job. Soon after, the man gave Grandfather a bad fright, and he suffered *espanto*. You understand what this is?"

"Some kind of weakness or sickness that hangs on," I answered.

"Exactly. It is caused by a sudden fright or some kind of shock," she finished. "Grandfather journeyed to another town to see a *curandera* for a ritual cleansing to rid him of the spirit that was dominating his body and sapping his strength, but the illness stayed with him. The *curandera* told him that a witch had put a hex on him. The next day Grandfather began the journey back to the mining camp. That night he and a friend camped by a stream. About midnight, as they sat by the fire, a big owl landed in the tree above their heads, watching them. Grandfather felt very ill and believed the owl was a *nagual,* a witch transformed into an animal. Sure that this was the witch that hexed him, following him to bring him to more harm, he took his friend's gun and shot it. It fell dead to the ground beneath the tree. Grandfather and his friend hurried over to it. The bullet had gone through the eye of the owl. When Grandfather got back to the mining camp, he was told that his enemy, the man who wanted his job, had left the camp the night before. The man was never seen again. So, Grandfather believed the man and the owl were the same witch."

Florinda made the sign of the cross, and I couldn't

help wondering how much of her grandfather's story she believed.

"I understand," I told her, glancing back into Trinidad's room at a small sound, but I couldn't see that the old man had moved. "He's so sick," I remarked, speaking more to myself than to Florinda.

"Father begged him," she said, "to go to the clinic, but he will not. Grandfather does not want to die among strangers in a place that is not his own."

I looked back once more at Trinidad. It might be the last time I would see him alive. Florinda suggested we find the others, and we walked through the front room and outside to the yard. Clay, Joe, and Cordelia stood near the goat pens, laughing and talking. We joined them, and after a few more minutes, we left. Unlike my conversation with Trinidad, Clay's talk with Joe had been a success. On the trip home, he filled me in on the details of the plan for bringing the people from the *ejidos* and pueblos into the vaccination scheme.

At first I paid attention, interested in the cleverness of the idea, Joe's idea, Clay said. But as we drove up the far side of a dry gulch, an owl, disturbed by our passing, sailed from a mesquite limb and flew into the distance, and I was reminded of Trinidad. He had killed an owl because he believed it to be a witch that had temporarily taken animal form. Had the disappearance afterward of the man who had wanted his job been coincidence, or could Trinidad have killed him, using the owl as justification or excuse, proof of the witchcraft being worked against him?

I knew better than to underestimate the powerful

influence of superstition. Like other folk wisdom, superstition is a form of cultural memory. Magic was very important to the Aztecs, Mayas, and Zapotecs. Maria Deed had always said that her Spanish-Indian heritage made her at ease with a world filled with spiritual phenomena.

I wanted Rhea's killer caught. That required uncovering the truth about how and why she died. I wondered if anyone had much chance of discovering the truth. Sooner or later, almost everyone in the area came in to shop at the trading post. I might, by tactful questioning, find out who had suffered such a run of bad luck or poor health that he might believe himself hexed.

Many of those who believed in the power of *curanderas* to heal also believed in the power of evil. Plenty of *curanderas* sold both cures and hexes. Trinidad had trusted in Rhea's power to heal. Yet he feared she had been killed because she was a witch. Why was he so sure? Why was he so afraid? I found myself wishing I had not left so soon, though I knew Trinidad was too sick to be pestered with questions.

"How did you find Trinidad?" Clay remarked. "Joe tells me his father's illness is grave."

I told him what had happened.

"It could be his illness making him so emotional, enlarging fears he might not have otherwise," Clay suggested.

As usual, I felt soothed just by talking things over with Clay. "Did Joe tell you about Hector's being in jail?" I asked as an afterthought.

"Yes, and I blame our immigration policy," he said, suddenly vehement. "Hector's like most of us, trying to provide for his family the best way he can. But as long as the United States allows Mexico to use this country as a safety valve for its overflow population, the corrupt *jefes* in Mexico City will sit on their asses instead of solving their country's problems, while men like Hector suffer for being caught in the middle.''

Clay punctuated his remark by shaking a finger in my general direction. As he did, I grabbed his waving hand.

''What happened to your hand? This looks like a bite.''

He shook his hand free and moved it back to the steering wheel. ''Just a little nip from one of Joe's dogs. I accidentally stepped on the poor mutt's tail,'' he said casually.

''The skin's broken.''

''Don't worry. I gave those two dogs their booster rabies shots last month.''

I sighed in relief. Few border families get vaccinations for their children, let alone livestock and working animals like Joe's dogs. In this, Joe is farsighted.

I turned in the seat to look again at Clay's injured hand where it rested on the steering wheel.

''I've been a fool,'' I cried.

''I'll still love you,'' Clay said, ''after you explain what you mean.''

''The Letter Man had a cut on his hand. I saw him scratching at it while we talked last night. And the timing. He took Linden Fonda's letter to Rhea. White Dog could have bitten him.''

I felt the forward surge of the pickup as Clay accelerated. "We'll go straight to his house. When did he deliver this letter?" he asked grimly.

"Lucy told me the letter arrived at the post office on the twenty-first. Glafiro took it to Rhea the next day."

I didn't have to ask if the rabies virus could have been active in White Dog on that date. I knew the answer was yes.

All I could do was close my eyes and pray that White Dog had been sick with anything but rabies. That if he did have the disease, we would find the Letter Man and get him to the clinic in time.

TEN

THE LETTER MAN wasn't home. His lean-to shed had
no door, merely an opening cut into the scrap lumber,
and we stepped inside. Glafiro's possessions were
few: a cot with a folded wool blanket, a wooden table
with dishes and an oil lamp, and beneath the table
two cardboard boxes, one containing neatly folded
clothes, the other holding religious pamphlets. The
packed-earth floor showed the striations from a recent sweeping with the broom in the corner.

"His pickup must have broken down again," I
said. "He could be anywhere."

"Let's check the barn," Clay said.

Glafiro had built his tiny shelter onto what had
once been a stone barn belonging to a vast private
holding, now carved up into an *ejido* system of small
communal farms and ranches that barely produced a
subsistence living.

The stone barn had one standing wall with the remaining three sides collapsed. Against the standing
wall, Glafiro had built a large coop for his chickens
and an even bigger pen for a few goats, unique struc-
tures displaying much ingenuity in utilizing old lumber, rocks, and used wire. Stacked tires lined with
straw served as nests for the hens. Overhead, goat-
skins stitched together and stretched on sotol *latillas*
provided shade.

The animal feeders—cut metal drums—stood

empty. Clay looked around, lifted a large rock from the top of an upright drum, and pulled out two feed sacks a little more than half full. He filled the feeder for the chickens, then the goats, then rolled the tops of the sacks closed and dropped them inside the drum. He replaced the rock that kept varmints from scavenging.

"I'm going to check outside," he said.

I remained in the barn and looked around. Against the remains of the long outside wall, Glafiro had his kitchen, a fifty-gallon drum with sand in the bottom on which to build the charcoal fire. I lifted the lid of a coffeepot on top of the drum. Empty. I reached into the hole cut in the side of the drum for loading the charcoal. No warmth rose from the ashes. Glafiro hadn't cooked today.

"His water barrel is full," Clay was saying as he came around the corner carrying a jug of water. He filled the bowls for the chickens and topped up the water in the trough for the goats.

"So we know he hasn't gone for water," I said, "and his pickup wasn't in town."

"He's out there somewhere." Clay stood staring west into the lowering sun that washed Mexico's Chihuahuan desert with golden light. Somewhere in that khaki-colored landscape the Letter Man might be sharing fresh tortillas with a family to which he delivered mail. If his pickup had broken down in the empty miles between the small ranching communities, he might spend the night in the vehicle, waiting until morning to walk in.

"What do we do now?" I asked.

"We go get Billy Deed."

We got into the pickup and drove back across the river to the constable's office, a silver trailer behind the post office. Billy had inherited his parents' ranch, which lies three miles southeast of El Polvo, but he often sleeps in the trailer. When the constable is needed, a call to the post office is passed to him quickly by Lucy Ramos or one of her children or grandchildren.

We parked alongside Billy's pickup. Billy came to the door, welcoming us with a smile.

When he heard what Clay had to say, a serious and worried look replaced the smile. He glanced at the sky. "Too bad there's no moon tonight, but I've got a couple of good hours of light left. I'll cross over and see if I can pick up Glafiro's tracks. Those bald tires of his should make tracking him easy if I can find his route. If I don't find him, I'll take along my bedroll and sleep in my pickup at his shed. Sooner or later he'll either drive or walk in."

Clay decided to join Billy in the search. I agreed to alert Lucy at the post office about what had happened so she could get the word out by telephone that it was urgent for Glafiro to contact Billy or come to the trading post as soon as possible.

"I'll walk," I told Clay when he offered to drop me at home. I watched the two pickups drive away, dust flying from the tires as first Billy and then Clay turned onto the road and headed back to the crossing. The high peaks of Mexico had never seemed so distant to me as they did now, knowing somewhere out there, miles from nowhere, Glafiro went unaware of his danger because I had failed to use my head and make an obvious connection between his injured hand and White Dog.

After leaving Lucy with the telephone in her hand, I crunched across the gravel and sand toward the trading post, the noise of my footsteps the only sound, until from behind one of the houses a dog whined and then howled. An omen? Something had wakened bad fortune for our community, and the trouble multiplied. "There will be another death," Doña Aurora had said. Would it be Glafiro's?

Outside the trading post, I stopped to help a woman from one of the ranches pry off a bent gas cap so she could fill the tank. I told her about the search for Glafiro and she promised to pass the word along, but I knew it was on the other side where we needed help, and there, among the *ejidos* and pueblos without telephones and electricity, it was Glafiro on whom we normally relied to pass the word.

Inside, there were no customers. Charlie sat in a chair behind the counter reading. He looked up, gave me a searching look, and asked, "Anything wrong?"

I told him about the search for Glafiro, and he offered to take his Cadillac out and scout around. I said Billy and Clay were doing all that could be done this late in the day, but that tomorrow, if we had not found Glafiro, his help would be needed.

The woman came in to pay for her gas. As she left, several children scampered through the doors, swarmed the soda cooler, bought candy, and settled themselves on the porch with the dog that accompanied them. The trading post stayed busy, but I felt hollow. Leaving Charlie to cope, I abandoned my place behind the counter and went into our living quarters. I heated a cup of water in the microwave and stirred in instant hot chocolate mix, took my cup to the table, and sat gazing out the window at the desert, a usually soothing exercise for putting things into perspective. But not this time. My eyes were drawn to the material on rabies that Clay had left lying on the table. I shuffled through the papers until I came to the document detailing the disease in man. Punishing myself, I read it, reinforcing what I knew already.

Rabies in a human being can incubate in as short a time as two days or as long as two years. The early symptoms—fever, nausea, sore throat, and depression or nervousness—are vague enough to be taken for flu. Even a physician may fail to diagnose the cause correctly since symptoms can be mistaken for appendicitis or inflammation of the pelvis or kidneys. By the time more obvious and serious symptoms appear it is too late. Seizures, excruciatingly painful spasms of the jaw and throat, uncontrollable hyperactivity, are followed by coma, then death in from two to eight days. Truly a hideous way to die. I tossed aside the information sheet. I felt like weeping. Where was Glafiro? Lost. Who could find lost things?

I jumped up so fast I knocked over my chair, grabbed my keys from the rack, and ran out the back door to the pickup. I had roared halfway up the road toward Doña Aurora's house before I realized I'd left without a word to Charlie.

Doña Aurora met me at the door, her tiny figure bundled in a sweater and wrapped with a shawl, though the temperature was mild, the chill of night an hour away.

"I knew you were coming," she said as I followed her inside. She sat down heavily at the table in front of the Virgin of Guadalupe and motioned me to a seat.

I tried to speak, but she put me off with a gesture. On the table in front of her a glass jar half-filled with water reflected the flame of the burning candle next to it. Doña Aurora took a vial from her pocket, removed the stopper, and poured a trickle of the contents into the water in the jar. It floated and had an iridescent sheen.

She looked into the jar. "The person you seek is on the other side. I see a small arroyo, and on a flat above, halfway up a slope, an adobe. It is whitewashed. There is a corral nearby made of juniper posts and sotol pickets." She sighed and looked up at me.

I felt deflated. How in all of northern Mexico was I to find one white adobe among the many scattered across the desert? The wandering trail Glafiro traveled delivering the mail probably covered two hundred miles.

As if reading my thoughts, Doña Aurora turned back to stare again at the swirling iridescence. "At the beginning of the arroyo you will find a shrine erected in memory of a child drowned when the arroyo flooded. It is a cross marked with the word *angelito* and the three letters *E.P.D.*"

"*En Paz Descanse*," I said. The equivalent of "Rest in Peace." Doña Aurora nodded.

"Thank you," I said, rising to my feet.

"You will find what you seek," she said. I took it as a blessing.

In less than five minutes I was back at the trading post scribbling a note for Clay. I left it propped on the table and went to the front to tell Charlie where I was going. As soon as I described the adobe and shrine, Charlie interrupted me.

"I've seen that cross," he said.

I seized him by his shoulders. "Can you find the place again?"

"I think so."

"Let's go. We'll take my pickup."

We put away the cash box, locked the front doors, and went out the back. I tossed the keys to Charlie. "You drive," I told him, grinning at the surprised look on his face.

Charlie took the river crossing where the body of the illegal had been found. I refrained from asking questions about where the shrine might be and left it to Charlie. He drove with little hesitation over a succession of ridges, making good time. Only the sound of the engine disturbed the silence of the earth. At last we dipped into a wide arroyo and pulled up the far side in a burst of acceleration. Charlie said, "This is it." From the top of the bank we had, in the last light, a view across the miles. Charlie braked to a stop, jumped out, and walked along the ridge for several feet. I climbed out and hurried after him. Near a creosote bush that almost covered it was the shrine, just as Doña Aurora had described it.

I glanced at Charlie. "Where's the house?" I asked.

He pointed off to the right. "It's there."

I strained my eyes and thought or imagined I saw a pale square shape.

We got back in the pickup. Charlie drove to within fifty feet of the adobe and stopped. There was no horse or burro in the corral, and no one in sight. Chickens roosted on the ridge of the roof, preparing to spend the coming night safe from coyotes. A wisp of smoke curled from a tin pipe jutting out of a corner of the roof. Someone was home.

I stepped out, cupped my hands around my mouth, and called out, "*¡Hola!* Is anyone in the house?"

The chickens fluttered at the noise and resettled themselves. The door opened a crack, spilling out a thin line of lamplight. A face peered at us around the door. "Are you lost?" a woman's voice asked.

"We are looking for someone," I explained. "We hope to find the Letter Man, Señor Paredes. We have an important message for him."

She opened the door, revealing three barefoot children clinging to her skirts. She was slight, dressed in a cotton skirt and blouse.

"You have found him. He is eating his supper. Come in," she said graciously.

Glafiro was too polite to show surprise at our appearance. He explained that his truck had broken down some miles from the señora's house and he had left it and walked here. The kind señora had offered to feed him before he walked back to his pickup to spend the night. Tomorrow or the next day, when her husband returned, perhaps he would be able to help Glafiro start the truck, or loan him a burro to get home.

We explained to Glafiro why we had come. He

looked at his hand and held it up to the light. "You see, my hand is healed. It is true that White Dog bit me. It was the day I took the letter, as you say. Señora Fair sometimes kept the dog tied with a rope around his neck and the other end tied to a stake in the ground. That day, the dog had pulled up the stake and dragged it and the rope until the stake caught in the crevice of a rock. The dog had exhausted himself trying to get free and lay whimpering. I untied the rope from his neck, and that is when he whirled and bit me, then ran away. Señora Fair saw this and made me scrub the wound with soap."

When I gently insisted that he must have an injection to be safe, he shrugged and said, "Surely, Señora Texana, my fate is not in my hand, but in the hands of God."

With a tortilla, he wiped his plate clean of beans, thanked his hostess, and turned to Charlie and me. "I will go back with you as you wish. I know you do what you think is good for me."

On the drive back we stopped at Glafiro's shed and picked up Billy, then drove to the trading post, where the lights burned brightly and Clay sat waiting on the porch. He paused only long enough to call ahead to the Texas Department of Health clinic and tell them we were coming. In a caravan of three we made the winding, fifty-mile drive to Presidio.

It was nearly midnight when Glafiro rolled up his sleeve and a male nurse administered two shots, the immune globulin and a rabies vaccination to trigger the body's immune system.

As the nurse tossed the used syringe into the garbage and Glafiro rolled his shirtsleeve back into place, I leaned against the wall, suddenly overcome by fatigue and nerves.

When Billy and Clay, with Glafiro between them and trailed by Charlie, walked down the corridor toward the glass doors, I held back, giving myself time to control my emotions.

Staring after them, the nurse said, "It will be interesting to see whether we got it in time."

I looked at him. "Fascinating," I said. I doubt he noticed the sarcasm.

ELEVEN

IN THE USUALLY quiet hour before dawn I wakened to thunder and the drumming of rain on the roof. A tin roof amplifies the sound and intensity of the rain, giving the illusion of abundance. In reality, our rainfall is the subject of jokes: "A fifteen-inch rainfall means the drops fall fifteen inches apart," or "We get ten inches of rain a year, and you ought to be here the day it falls." This shower ended in a few minutes and I slept again, to wake tired and ravenous.

Clay had breakfast on the table. We ate his homemade waffles and watched the rising sun reflected in the millions of raindrops caught in the scrub and cacti that dot the ridge tops.

After I swallowed the last bite of my third waffle, Clay reached across the table and patted my hand. "Get dressed," he said. "I've got a surprise for you."

"What? I hate surprises."

"We're going up to the Darke Ranch. I meant to tell you last night, but the search for Glafiro drove it out of my mind. Robert Darke invited us to see the dig."

Feeling testy, I said, "Robert's pet archaeologist earning his keep."

With humor in his voice Clay said, "Does that make me Robert's pet vet?"

As Clay had intended, the silly joke made me laugh and restored my good humor.

"Can Charlie stay and keep the trading post open?" I asked. I decided we needed a day of pleasant diversion.

"Already taken care of."

"Then I'll get ready. I may even put on makeup for the occasion," I said, smiling at my husband and suddenly looking forward to the day.

Robert Darke expected us about nine o'clock, Clay explained, so we had some time to kill. He went out to his trailer to feed the goat I had bought and put out oats for a burro he had been tending for over a week. I took my time in the shower, washed my hair, carefully applied more makeup than I'd worn in ages, dressed in slacks and a matching jacket instead of my usual jeans, and put on sturdy shoes for the rough walking I anticipated we might do. Ready for the day, I went out to tell Charlie how much I appreciated his help, then joined Clay at the pickup. We decided to go in separate vehicles in case he wanted to stay and discuss additions to the plan for the rabies vaccination drive with Robert, or more likely Lank, since the ranch manager would be the working partner in the scheme.

As we pulled away from the trading post, we passed three men whose round faces were tanned to the color of leather, driving a pack of burros across the empty road by whacking them on the rump with stout sticks. The animals were loaded with bulging burlap bags, probably filled with *candelilla* wax, which I buy, paying slightly higher rates than the gatherers would get in Mexico. I declare the wax through customs in Presidio and ship it to be refined in Alpine. The finished product is used in cosmetics and polishes. I waved a hand at the men, technically smugglers since it is illegal for them to sell the wax outside of Mexico, though I break no law in buying it. Satisfied that Charlie, canny in all things of the border, would handle the transaction, I did not stop.

I accelerated to catch up to Clay and lowered the window to enjoy the cool, crisp air and the sharp, medicinal tang of the creosote plants, the scent accentuated by the moisture from the brief rain.

We turned off the road and slowed to take the track that led past the path to Rhea's house. Resolutely, I put all thoughts of the murder out of my mind and looked straight ahead as we began the steady ascent into the mass of the volcanic mountains.

Ranches in our region, spread over multiples of thousands of acres, seldom come on the market. The Darke family has owned their land for three generations. The main house lies in a grassy basin wrapped by the mountains. Built in a horseshoe shape, the house is flanked by copies of pre-Columbian art, the originals owned by Robert and reproduced here in heroic size. Designed by an architect, the house has monolithic walls interspersed with sheets of glass that frame portions of the 360-degree views.

The owner of all this stood in the wide, almost ceremonial entrance. Robert is a handsome man in his mid-fifties with white hair and dark eyes. Only the mouth hints at a tendency to petulant weakness that can surface if the man is crossed. Dressed in faded jeans starched and pressed to a military crease, a suede shirt, and ostrich-skin boots, with three cream-colored Great Pyrenees dogs lolling at his feet, Robert and his setting provided a picture worthy of *Architectural Digest*.

As we came to a stop, he strode from the entrance, dogs swarming with him, and shouted, "Welcome, welcome. Get out and we'll ride up to the site together."

The dogs greeted us with lavish abandon, and Robert took my arm and guided me to a white Suburban. He keeps five for the use of his guests, trading them in yearly for new models—same color, same interior. White is the color of choice for vehicles in our hot country, where summer temperatures regularly top 100 degrees. Clay got in behind me. Robert shooed away the dogs, climbed behind the wheel, and circled around the house and past the landing strip, taking us out of the basin.

As Robert drove, he talked, turning his head to look at me or Clay with every other comment.

"You're going to love this. The discovery we made was a surprise, even to Eliot, and of real archaeological significance. We're going to make news with this find."

"I don't suppose you're going to tell us the details until we get there," I said, knowing how much Robert enjoyed the drama of such a moment.

He smiled at me, his charm as bright and perfect as his teeth. He's good one-on-one, Clay had said after meeting Robert for the first time sixteen years ago. Clay and I, too, had met that day, at one of the fiestas, introduced by Robert's wife Number Two. Number Three had since come and gone. Robert's marriages begin with a rush of affection, last about three years, and terminate in lawsuits.

"Your husband," Robert said to me while turning around to include Clay in his approving glance, "really did a fine job on one of my saddle horses."

"I never asked you how the animal was injured," Clay said.

"We're not sure, but we think a smuggler must have taken the animal out. The first of the month, one of the hands riding the south fence line noticed the fence leaning. He got down to investigate and found that someone had sawed off three fence posts at the base. The tracks, very faint, of a horse and one person crossing over were still there. Whoever it was flattened the fence to lead the horse across, then propped the posts back in place to delay our finding the damage. Lank thinks the horse might have thrown the man, run, and got cut jumping back over the fence at some point," Robert explained. "I'm just glad the animal is okay. I'd hate to lose a good saddle horse."

"The south fence line?" I asked. I was thinking of the dead illegal by the river. Could he have been headed south and stolen Robert's horse? It might explain how he'd died. The horse balked and threw him, he cracked his head, made it as far as the river, and died while the horse ran for home.

"Is this the horse Lank called Billy Deed about?" I asked.

"I called him after Lank reported to me about the fence," Robert said.

"When did you first miss the horse?" I thought I

kept my voice easy, but Clay looked over at me and smiled.

This time Robert turned to look at me as he answered and the Suburban veered left, bouncing over rocks. "We can't be sure," he said, steering the vehicle back onto the ranch road. "The horses are grazing in the big trap. Twice a week a man replaces the bales in the feeders. He noticed the animal missing on the thirty-first, but we don't know when it got out. It wasn't until the second of this month that Lank found the horse grazing with the some of the cattle."

Clay said, "According to Lank, by the time he found the horse the cut on its leg had partially healed but gaped open because it needed stitches."

I thought that the next time I spoke to Andalon, I'd mention these things.

Robert had turned up the draw that he said would take us to the site of the excavations. I wondered what we would see. Over the summer and fall, when the various members of Eliot Lofts' team had come into the trading post, I had heard snippets of conversation about an unexpected discovery. I have an interest in such things and keep a display in the trading post of fossils, stone tools and weapons, and pottery, most of which have been brought to me from the other side and bartered for supplies. At least that way the artifacts stay here instead of disappearing down the highway, removed by amateurs either to sell or put in private collections or taken by professionals for study or display in museums.

Robert maneuvered up a slope and over a rutted ridge top into a half-mile-wide expanse of brush crisscrossed with dry stream beds that in the far distance braided together to become Waller Creek.

"We're going up there." Robert pointed northwest toward a clearly rutted track made by the team's daily trekking in and out.

Two miles and ten minutes later, we arrived and parked beside two other white Suburbans nosed in against a hillside slashed by a thick exposure of rock overhang.

The wind had picked up, whipping around us as we got out. Eliot Lofts emerged from the shadow of the rock, his thick yellow hair lifting around his face like feathers. "You're here. Good, good," he said expansively. "We have everything ready for you." He made an inviting gesture toward the shadows and I saw that the overhang hid the entrance to a cave.

"Sábado Cave," said Robert. "Discovered by my grandfather as a boy and named for the day of the week on which he found it."

The long, wide opening of the cave faced south. Near the lip of the entrance a portable generator stood under a tarp. Nearby a table was spread with artifacts and excavation tools and surrounded by four folding metal chairs. Lofts stepped aside to let Robert lead the way, but the archaeologist did the talking as we entered the cave.

"My team and I started excavating last year in an exposure of sedimentary rock. It was Robert's idea to excavate the cave."

"I used to find arrow points in here when I was a boy," Robert said.

"He has all the instincts of an archaeologist," Lofts told us.

The strung lights and high ceiling of the cave made our descent easy, but as we moved downward the rocky floor narrowed and the walls gradually closed in until the ceiling was only head-high. In this small space of dark shadows and spotlighted areas, the four team members worked with barely enough room to keep from bumping into each other.

Lofts made the introductions. "Mrs. Jones—"

"Texana, please," I corrected him.

"Texana, you know the team. Mr....ah...Clay, this fellow in the corner working on one of the fire hearths is Kirk Anderson. The young lady with the brush is Mattie Brant. Roy Hammit is there by the stratigraphy markers, ready to show you the zones. And Jessica...where?"

A tall angular figure moved out of a dark corner.

"This is Jessica Rex, a very talented photographer. She takes the site photos. We must record each artifact from three viewpoints. She also takes candid shots of everything as we work, for—" Jutting his eyebrows upward in a question, he peered around me at Robert.

Robert said, "We have a book project in the making."

Lofts said, "Didn't want to spoil the surprise."

I had taken Jessica Rex for a man when she first moved into the light. Her cropped hair—probably a very expensive cut, I realized—added to the mannish impression, but her face was that of a classic beauty. Dressed in a long-sleeved khaki shirt and slacks, and holding a camera with a flash, she acknowledged our presence with a fleeting smile and a glance from beneath downcast eyes that gave an impression of shyness. No makeup, no nail polish, but flawless skin and eyes of deep blue. Ignoring us, she put aside the camera she held and busied herself with a second one, set on a tripod and resting near what Lofts had called a hearth. I realized that while I had been observing the photographer, Lofts had been talking.

"...and as the dig progressed we knew we had found some of the earliest, perhaps *the* earliest Native Americans," Lofts was saying as he pointed to the stratigraphy markings and put his finger on a spot head-high and marked with a lettered card. "This is the floor level of the original cave. We excavated one square meter at a time. These little lettered cards are the level markings. At the lowest level we're finding animal bones, flint tools, arrow points—things which indicate that man was here thirty thousand years ago."

"That's only so far," Robert said. "Eliot expects to find more at deeper levels."

"We're shipping the bones to a paleontologist in El Paso," Lofts added.

We spent an hour in the cave, watching Kirk Anderson uncover a fresh artifact, a large bone with an arrow point sticking in it. Jessica Rex photographed it in place before Kirk removed it for further photographing, cleaning, and cataloging. Clay and I oohed and ahed at appropriate moments, but our appreciative noises couldn't match either Lofts' genuine enthusiasm or Robert's near-expert knowledge. I began to understand why amateurs paid to work with Lofts.

While Robert and Clay listened to Lofts expand upon his subject, Mattie Brant showed me a box of artifacts already marked for cataloging. As I sorted through the points and tools and bits of bone, a flash went off almost under my nose, startling me so that I jumped backward and bumped my head against the cave wall.

"Sorry," I heard Jessica say as spots danced before my eyes. Clay's hand found my elbow and I moved forward with his guidance.

Lofts said, "Jessica can't resist snapping pictures. Perhaps she'll make you famous with that shot."

"I prefer to be asked before my picture is taken," I said, trying to resume my dignity.

"Candid photos are so much better," Jessica said. "If I announce I'm going to take a photo, the subject goes all self-conscious and stiff. This way, the subject is relaxed and the emotion I want to capture shows on the face instead of that dead I'm-having-my-picture-taken expression. You looked great. Inquisitive and intelligent, and so intent on the artifacts. You'll see. I'll give you a print."

"I'd sure like a copy," Clay said.

No longer blinded by the effect of the flash, I could see Jessica nod, then busy herself once again with the camera.

Robert stretched out his arms as if to enfold us and announced, "Time for us to get back to the house. Eliot, we'll see all of you there in a few minutes. Jessica, will you ride with us?"

"I'll come on my own."

"As you like," Robert said.

I caught Clay's eye. Hard not to notice the singling out of Jessica Rex. And we weren't the only ones to notice. From her worktable Mattie Brant gave Robert a look of such wistfulness that it shocked me to see the sudden switch to loathing as her eyes turned to Jessica.

Robert moved toward the entrance and we followed. I reflected that, given the Mattie-Jessica-Robert triangle, the rest of the morning might be very awkward.

All the way back, Robert talked of the dig and its potential to rewrite the books on the archaeology of the United States. He parked at the entrance to the house, and we were instantly welcomed by the dogs, bushy tails wagging, massive heads nodding to be petted. Accompanied by the dogs, we passed through the double front doors, which were carved in Mexico, and entered Robert's home. The living area was baronial in size, with a few fine antiques and many Turkish rugs that softened the tinted concrete floors.

Immediately before us a series of tables along a section of the wall held the most prized and important artifacts from the cave excavations. Framed color photographs hung above. These were not workmanlike pictures taken as a recording tool of the project, but works of art. In the extreme closeups of fossilized bones, points, tools, and pottery shards, form and color dominated, transforming the artifacts into abstractions.

"Fine, aren't they," Robert commented.

"They're beautiful," I said, meaning it.

"I'm glad you like my work," Jessica Rex said from behind us. I turned in time to see Robert lean in and kiss her cheek in welcome while she slipped a slim-fingered hand over his arm. Identical in height, both handsome and healthy, with a well-bred look that sometimes comes with wealth, they made an attractive couple.

"You're obviously an expert photographer," Clay said. "Are you an archaeologist, too?"

"Just an interested amateur," Jessica replied.

"She has taken some remarkable photographs of local people," Robert said proudly. "We'll show them to you after we eat."

A middle-aged Mexican woman I knew as Luisa entered from the dining room and offered us coffee in delicate cups from a tray.

We sipped the aromatic brew and made small talk about the ranch and Robert's plans for this year's fiesta until Eliot Lofts and the others arrived and we moved into the dining room, where Luisa had laid out a splendid brunch of cheese frittata, crusty bread, and fruit. The meal concluded with a champagne toast by Robert to "the successful work of Eliot and his team." This was followed by an eloquent homage from Eliot Lofts "to Robert, our spiritual and financial mentor."

As we walked back to the living room, I found myself beside Jessica.

"The other photographs Robert mentioned," I said, "I'm looking forward to seeing them."

"I took them for my own amusement," she said casually. "I used them to try out a new developing process. It gives an unusual finish."

"Have you been working with the team long?" I asked. "I haven't seen you around El Polvo."

"I don't have much free time," she said.

Ahead of us, Robert walked with Mattie, who listened to what he was saying with a rapt expression on her face.

"Excuse me, please," Jessica said to me. She caught up to Robert and Mattie, who looked resentful at having her tête-à-tête with Robert interrupted. Jessica made a remark too low for anyone else to hear. Robert nodded and smiled, and Jessica left us.

In the living room we broke into smaller groups. I joined Mattie at one end of the room, while Clay took the opportunity to corner Robert about the rabies project. Lofts listened to their conversation for a few minutes, then turned to Kirk and Ray and talked shop.

I learned from Mattie that she was from Abilene and an only child. She had graduated college with a teaching certificate but had found after one semester in the classroom that she hated teaching. She had spent her savings to work with Lofts in a field where, as she phrased it, "I can work alone with inanimate things that don't talk back." After this burst of information she grew silent, and I filled the gap by asking her about Jessica Rex.

Jessica, according to Mattie, came from San Antonio, had a rich stepmother and a doting, elderly father, loved nothing but herself, and had met Robert at a charity ball. Without effort she had assumed a place in his affections as her right.

I tried to soothe Mattie's jealousy with a suggestion. "People usually enjoy being flattered."

She ducked her head. "I can't do things like that. I don't know how."

"If you admire him, let him know."

She shook her head.

Raising his voice slightly, Robert announced, "Jessica's working in the darkroom, but she said I might show you the special photos she's taken as a study of the borderland. Come along with me."

We followed him into a smaller room off the gallery that served as a library. Several neat stacks of mounted photos were on a circular table in the center of the room.

Mattie stayed by the door. The rest of us moved to the table.

"Look through these," Robert said. "You'll see what a talent Jessica has."

I picked up the top picture from one stack and, enchanted, another and another. In two series, one of landscapes, the other portraits, Jessica Rex had recorded the wonderful melding of the two disparate worlds that meet at the Rio Grande. The landscapes captured the kaleidoscopic colors of the desert, from the pale purple of twilight settling over the river to the shadowless hot light of midday.

Clay summed up our reactions to the portraits. "These aren't photos. They're works of art."

Robert stood looking over my shoulder as I held up a picture of a brown little boy eating a cerise ice pop.

"Jessica has a wonderful aesthetic sense, don't you agree?" Robert said.

I lifted the next picture. "It's Rhea Fair," I said more loudly than I intended. Clay gave my shoulder a squeeze.

"Was that her first name, Rhea?" Robert said. "I don't think I ever heard anyone call her anything but Mrs. Fair. Jessica took that photo last spring. She accompanied me when I visited with Mrs. Fair about marketing a line of her herbal cures. I thought it would help her out financially, but she wasn't interested. Jessica snapped the picture just as we were leaving."

Rhea stood in the doorway of the line shack, White Dog sitting at her feet, gazing up at her.

"An interesting study," Eliot Lofts said. "Though the lady looks a bit tense."

"Mrs. Fair had a natural reticence in dealing with people," Robert said. "I think Jessica captured perfectly the spirit of the woman."

"I can't wait to see the picture she took of Texana," Clay said.

"I admit, I've never liked having my picture taken, but this time, I'm glad I did," I said.

Robert smiled at us all, pleased that we appreciated Jessica's talent as much as he did. Reluctantly, I suggested it was time for me to get back and relieve Charlie. Robert accompanied Clay and me outside to say good-bye. Clay told me he planned to stop at Lank Carter's house. When I drove away, Robert still leaned against the truck talking to Clay.

The drive home was uneventful. I checked in with Charlie and asked about the wax gatherers. He had made a good bargain, with half the purchase price in feed oats, matches, and canned goods. I went to the kitchen to grill a steak for him.

While Charlie sat at a table slicing up the twenty-four-ounce steak and swirling the pieces through the pool of bottled steak sauce on his plate, I waited on three customers buying gas and turned down a man who wanted to sell me a Texas lyre snake and a mottled rock rattler.

Two hours later, Clay drove in. I glanced out front to make sure no one had driven up to the gas pumps before joining him in the kitchen where he was already pouring a glass of tea.

He turned around smiling and said, "Will you go first or shall I?"

"You."

"The lady photographer has a golden eye."

"And she's struck gold with Robert, don't you think?"

"Loves her, loves her art," Clay said.

"Is she going to be the next trophy wife?

"I'd say so, though Robert didn't. Not to me, anyway."

"Mattie Brant adores him."

Clay shook his head. "Hasn't a chance. Too small, too dark, too gauche. Each of Robert's wives has been a slick, leggy blonde."

"Jessica is certainly beautiful."

"And talented."

"That photo of the *curandera* showed so much more than Rhea ever revealed about herself. She looked so vulnerable."

"Maybe," Clay said, "you're seeing something that's not there. Something you feel because you knew her."

"I'm beginning to wonder how well any of us *really* knew her."

TWELVE

LATE FRIDAY afternoon the Department of Health lab notified Clay of the test results on the head of the coyote: positive for rabies. He had no hope that when the tests came back on White Dog, probably on Monday or Tuesday, the results would be different.

Saturday morning he left before daylight on a circuit of ranches with livestock that needed vaccinating. He carried with him a list of possibly exposed animals: eight cows, one goat, one horse, four dogs, and one cat. Since the health department's mandate dictates that unvaccinated animals be destroyed, I knew Clay faced an unpleasant day's work. With him had gone Charlie, driving my pickup loaded with cages to hold stray dogs or cats, or pets only suspected of exposure and thus to be held in quarantine.

I spent all day behind the counter selling mostly gas, cold six-packs of beer, candy, and soft drinks, and monitoring the children who congregate on the front porch all day. At ten o'clock I walked to the post office and left my lotto number and money for the ticket with Lucy, who would hand them over, along with numbers from half a dozen other people, to Everett Barron. After unloading his postal van, Everett would take the numbers back to Marfa, purchase the tickets, and leave them with Lucy on his next trip. Everett lives in confident expectation of a big tip should any of us hit the magic six. Since the mountains block out radio and TV reception, he also brings word of the winning numbers, which Lucy posts on the bulletin board beside the FBI's Most Wanted list.

Around noon, a young woman and four wide-eyed children came in, shoes in hand and feet caked with mud from having waded across the river from an *ejido*. The mother carried a basket with a puppy in it. She held out the basket toward me, pointed to the pup, and explained that it could not swallow. She wanted the animal doctor to clear whatever had lodged in its throat.

I told the children to have a soft drink on the house, took the woman around back to the trailer, opened a cage, and asked her to place the puppy inside. I closed and locked the cage, then explained that the problem the puppy had swallowing was a sign of illness. "Have the children," I asked, "played with the puppy?" Not only had all four children been around the animal constantly, but the mother also told me how she had put her hand in its mouth to try and clear its throat. After I explained to her that all the family needed shots to keep from getting sick themselves, I called Lucy Ramos, who called one of her sons to come and drive the mother and children to the clinic. The mother kept shaking her head and saying no to me, so I called Lucy a second time and she came in person to talk to the tearful woman. It took a half hour of persuasive pleading on Lucy's part before the mother finally agreed to the necessity of the unwelcome and frightening trip.

By the time mother and children had climbed into

Lucy's son's pickup and headed down the road, I felt drained. I hung the "Back at" sign on the front doors—without bothering to write in a time—and went to the kitchen, poured a glass of tea, and stirred in lemon juice out of the bottle and a teaspoon of sugar. Before I could take the first sip, the telephone rang.

"Rhea Fair's body is being released for burial," Andalon said without preamble. We know each other well enough not to feel the necessity of small talk.

"Who to?"

"The funeral home in Alpine. The priest offered to handle arrangements since, as bail jumpers, her sons are unlikely to show up on this side. Not that anybody is asking to get them back," he added dryly.

"I guess they know she's dead?"

"I telephoned Matt the day after you found the body."

"I always thought Luke cared more about his mother than Matt did," I said.

"Maybe, but I couldn't reach Luke, and Matt claimed not to know where I might locate his brother."

"Any other news?"

I could almost hear Andalon smile. "You want to know about the autopsy on the Mexican national," he said obligingly.

I pounced on it. "Well?"

"I won't have anything until Tuesday or Wednesday."

"I have some information for you." I proceeded to tell him about the horse missing from the Darke Ranch during the days surrounding Rhea's death.

"Texana," he said when I finished. The more patient Andalon is being, the more precise his enunciation becomes. Now he chopped out syllables like an English teacher. "Any one of a hundred smugglers, thieves, or illegals could have cut that fence and taken that horse. There are coincidences. Not everything has to add up."

"There are too many coincidences surrounding Rhea's death, if you ask me. And I know you didn't," I snapped.

He continued as if I hadn't spoken. "Father Jack insists on going to Juarez to see what Matt wants done for his mother. I suggested he take you with him."

"Why?" I demanded.

"I want you to ask Matt about his mother and about the last time he saw her."

"You think he's the murderer?"

"He's too lazy, and there's no motive. At least, not one I know about," Andalon said thoughtfully. "Just talk to him. You're the most tenacious person I know. If there's something to find, you'll find it. Remember that time in seventh grade when somebody scraped the door of your father's new pickup and you found that infinitesimal dot of paint, saved it in a plastic bag, and went around comparing it to the paint on every vehicle that came into town until you found a match?"

"And as soon as I confronted Jody Carl he admitted scraping Daddy's pickup, in spite of you telling me I'd never find out who did it."

Andalon laughed at my flash of childhood resentment. "As long as you're going to follow—no, make that lead—this case," he said, "I might as well make good use of you."

I told him I'd think about it and talk to Father Jack. He knew full well I'd do it, but I saw no reason to admit my eagerness.

The rest of the afternoon passed uneventfully. At six, just as I was locking up, Clay and Charlie returned. Clay came inside looking exhausted and headed for the shower. I went outside to talk to Charlie, who was unloading dogs from several cages into the quarantine kennels that ran behind the trailer. Poor scared animals, I thought.

When Charlie had finished, I invited him to dine with us at La Casa Azul. He told me Clay had asked him already.

By the time I got back inside Clay had finished his shower and was stretched out on the bed asleep, his damp hair soaking the pillow. I took my shower and shampooed my hair. The sound of the blow dryer woke Clay and I could hear him moving around. When I came out of the bath, he had dressed in a soft yellow shirt and brown slacks. I put on a shirt-waist dress in sage green, stepped into my brown flats, and we went out the door.

Charlie, face scrubbed and wearing a gray suit that looked to be of the same fifties vintage as his car, waited by the Cadillac. He offered to drive, and we accepted. The Fleetwood is a wonderful car: smooth, powerful, and roomy enough inside to house a family of gypsies. Charlie kept to a sedate, driving-grandma speed and parked at a careful distance from the pickups lined up in front of the blue house. The restaurant has no identifying sign other than its vivid coat of paint, is open only on Thursday, Friday, and Saturday evenings from six until ten, sells no alcoholic beverages, and serves a limited but delicious menu of traditional Mexican dishes.

Inside, early diners crowded the one-room restaurant, and we had to wait briefly while the waiter wiped a table and seated us by the window overlooking a small courtyard with a birdbath in the center. The courtyard connects the restaurant to the kitchen and to the living quarters of Claudia and Ruben Reyes, cook and waiter respectively.

I looked around the room. At a table in one corner, Annie Luna and Billy Deed sat together looking slightly ill at ease with one another. At a center table, Robert Darke sat talking and smiling to a complacent-looking Jessica Rex. I noticed that the two extra chairs at their table had been removed and put against the wall by Ruben. Otherwise, waiting customers would have been seated with them. Apparently the lovers wanted a private conversation. The six other tables were filled with people from the ranches, including Lank Carter and his wife Nora with another couple. Before the restaurant closed, each table would have emptied and filled at least twice again, custom dictating that diners linger no longer than an hour so that everyone could be served.

Ruben took our order and brought large glasses of iced tea. We purposely avoided talk about rabies and discussed the shifting politics of Mexico, and Charlie entertained us with anecdotes of his travels. As we talked, sound bites of conversation from other tables floated to our ears: "…pointless to fence along the river when it will be cut every day… Why doesn't the state stop the dumping of New York sewer waste out here? Next it'll be nuclear waste, and then we'll really have riders of the purple sage.''

Ruben brought steaming plates of shredded beef enchiladas with red sauce to our table and refilled our glasses with tea. More customers came in, including Father Jack Raff.

Dressed in a black T-shirt, jeans, and running shoes, he looked more like an aging grad student than a priest. He stopped at the table nearest the door and visited for a few minutes with its occupants, then surveyed the room for an empty chair. Nodding and smiling at the room at large, he came to our table. Clay invited him to join us, and he sat down. Ruben took the priest's order and departed for the kitchen. Father Jack beamed at me.

''Er, Texana, I understand you're going with me to Juarez. It will be an, er, good thing. I don't know this young man personally and I understand you do.''

Clay looked questioningly at me, and I explained Andalon's suggestion, in a slightly amended version, then started to address the priest. ''Father—''

''Call me Jack,'' he interrupted. And before I could finish my sentence, he added that he'd be happy to drive and asked when we might leave. I told him I had to make arrangements about the trading post and I'd let him know.

''I have an idea, Jack,'' Clay said, putting down his fork. ''You know we're fighting a rabies outbreak?''

The priest looked grave and nodded.

''We want to involve the people on the other side, encourage everyone to get livestock and pets vaccinated. Joe Quiroz had a great idea for a fiesta with food, a band, games for the kids, prizes for livestock and pets, the whole shooting match. How about a blessing of the animals?''

''Er, a blessing of the animals? Yes, the Episcopalians do that a lot, you know.'' He leaned back in his chair and thought about it. ''I've been asked to do stranger things. Just last week I had to bless a house the owner believed had been hexed by a Jehovah's Witness. A blessing of the animals, eh? Yes, I can do that for you. The mothers and kids will like that. I'll write a blessing and make up some extra holy water. When will you need me?''

''Next Friday afternoon,'' Clay said. ''I've talked to the schoolteacher about letting the kids out at two o'clock. We can have the blessing first thing, and I'll be right there with the vaccine and needles.''

Ruben brought Father Jack's plate piled high with *carnitas,* small pieces of meat fried crisp on the outside, succulent on the inside, and served with tortillas and salsa.

During the rest of the meal, our conversation concerned the plans and logistics for the community fiesta. We concluded the evening with cups of coffee rich with cinnamon and brown sugar. Clay paid the bill, including Father Jack's, and as the priest had walked from his trailer by the church, Charlie drove him home.

After we got to the trading post and said good night to Charlie, Clay and I sat on the porch for a while looking up at the night sky. It was the dark of the moon, the stars were out, and a bright shooting star sailed through Cygnus.

"You do the driving to Juarez," Clay said, putting his arm around my shoulder. "That priest drives with his mind on God and his foot on the accelerator."

"You think I should go then?" I said, suddenly feeling deflated and unsure of everything.

"Why not? You want answers. You might get some from Matt."

What I love about my husband is that when I most doubt myself, he has the most confidence in me. I would go to Juarez and question Matt Fair.

THIRTEEN

EL PASO is the only major city in Texas on Mountain Standard time, so when Father Jack's Toyota tailed my pickup into the city limits at 1:15 on Monday afternoon, it was an hour later in the rest of the state.

We had made our plans for the trip on Sunday afternoon. I avoided riding with Father Jack by the expedient of also using the opportunity of being in El Paso to buy stock for the trading post, thus making it necessary that I drive my pickup. The priest quickly grasped the idea that it would consume less of his time if he drove his own vehicle so he could leave for home as soon as the conversation with Matt Fair was over.

We had made the three-hundred-mile trip in good time, with Father Jack maintaining a law-abiding car length behind me all the way. I had been good, venturing no more than ten miles per hour over the speed limit even in the long barren stretches of the interstate where we passed no one for miles except the occasional eighteen-wheeler hurtling by at a mile-lapping ninety.

I decided we would park on this side of the border and cross over the pedestrian bridge, since the priest's experience in driving in a border city was limited to the small villages near El Polvo and the more benign border town of Ojinaga. I doubted that Father Jack knew the cardinal rule for gringo drivers:

Never catch the eye of the traffic cop, and even if he chases your vehicle, ignore him. If he catches you, pretend you don't speak Spanish even if you're fluent. If he explains himself clearly, two dollars is plenty for the *mordita* or "bite" by which he pads his meager salary.

As we waited at a red light, I watched two immigration officers walking down a row of cars. As they neared a blue van, the doors burst open and like clowns at a circus twenty or thirty people tumbled out and ran, scattering in all directions and leaving the van blocking traffic just as the light changed. One officer gave halfhearted chase while the other spoke into a walkie-talkie and waited for his partner to work his way back. Across the Rio Grande the dirt roads and cardboard *colonias* of Juarez are carved into the rocky hillside and crowded with too many people with no direction to go except north.

With a population of a million and a half and still growing, Juarez dominates its sister city in size, color, and noise. In its earlier days, Juarez was so squalid that officials of the Mexican city kept their families in El Paso. Now, on the few paved streets, tourism flourishes for nicer reasons than the quickie divorce once synonymous with the city's name.

Father Jack followed me closely through the prosperous streets of El Paso and into a parking lot. We locked our vehicles and walked. At the Santa Fe Street border crossing, we were immediately caught up in a crush of people passing in both directions. At the end of the bridge a congregation of beggars—lame, blind, in carts, on crutches and able-bodied, holding pictures of Jesus—stridently pleaded over the lower pitch of the peddlers hawking cigarettes, gum, fruit, and trinkets. This was Avenida Juarez, a street of bars, curio shops, discos, and street vendors that leads to the city market, the plaza, and the cathedral.

The *avenida* was crowded with bargain-hunting tourists, and the air smelled of tortillas and stale cooking oil. Moving in and out among clumps of shoppers, street hustlers hawked cheap trinkets and pirated tapes. Father Jack and I worked our way through the crowds and past rows of paintings of Elvis on black velvet, embroidered dresses and shirts twisting on the breeze from hangers, stacks of pottery, and piñatas. As we neared the corner, a thin boy of fourteen or fifteen jumped in front of us, cajoling, "Need a Rolex, mister? Miss?" and dangling a watch under our noses as he danced backward. We ignored him, and he moved to another tourist.

Father Jack blinked and looked around. "Like Mardi Gras in New Orleans, isn't it? All puke and peddlers."

I laughed. "It gets livelier and louder at night when the musicians come out," I told him.

We turned off the *avenida* and onto a potholed street lined with less prosperous shops—many strung with lights—and unsavory bars. Packs of pathetically thin, mangy stray dogs roamed among the crowds. There were no numbers on the buildings and few signs, so I asked at several places until I found the shop belonging to Connie Chavez. Matt Fair's wife eyed us warily when we asked for him and pointed to a room behind the storefront.

Father Jack and I walked into the shadowy room

and found Matt, shoulders stooped, dirty hair tumbled in curls around the puffy face of the habitual drunkard, sitting at a table eating a bowl of *menudo*, a tripe soup that is a popular cure for hangover.

After one sharp look, Matt ignored us until he emptied the bowl. He took a lumpy cigarette from a tin on the table, lit it, and inhaled deeply, his eyes glittering slits. He shoved out a chair with his foot as an invitation to us to join him.

Father Jack stepped back to let me take the chair while he pulled up a stool from the corner. Other than the table, the room held a recliner, a television and VCR, and a stereo—all the comforts of the small-time drug dealer, and all smuggled in from the U.S. Near the window, someone had tacked up a picture torn from a magazine of Jack Nicholson as a border patrol agent.

I placed the paper bag I had brought with me onto the table. Matt opened it and bent his head to peer inside. His eyes widened and he turned the bag upside down and smiled as eight cellophane-wrapped packages of chocolate-frosted cupcakes tumbled onto the table. For an instant, as he grinned, Matt looked the way I remembered him, a mischievous boy a few years behind me in school.

"You used to like those," I said to him.

"As a bribe, it's not much." He turned to stare at Father Jack. "How about you? Did you bring a sweetener?" he said, rubbing his fingers together, "or just a sermon?"

The priest dipped his head as if he might butt Matt with it and answered with more asperity than I would have credited him with having. "The county is paying for your mother's funeral and the church is donating its services. I think that's sufficient generosity for the day."

An expression of shame and anger crossed Matt's face. "Andalon said you'd be coming. What do you want to know?" he asked.

"What would you like done for your mother? The kind of service? She was not, I am given to understand, a Catholic."

"Say whatever mumbo jumbo you like over her," Matt said, sucking on the cigarette and exhaling slowly. "You know, a Mass."

"You misunderstand—" the priest began.

Matt cut him off by getting to his feet and going into the kitchen. He returned with a bottle of clear liquid and three glasses. He put a glass in front of each of us, poured. I recognized the smell: sotol, a potent liqueur distilled from the sotol plant. Matt lifted his glass and emptied it in one swallow. I touched my glass to my lips but didn't swallow. I'd had my first taste of the stuff with Andalon when I was sixteen. I recalled the smooth feel on the tongue, the warm swallow, the bite in the stomach. After that it had not been friendly. Father Jack picked up his glass, evidently not his first taste as he took the whole glass at a gulp without choking or turning red in the face. He stopped Matt from pouring another by turning the glass down.

Matt looked sideways at me, jerked his head at Father Jack, and said, "I know why he's here. What about you?"

"Er, Mr. Fair—" the priest said.

Matt swiveled his head around. "Your job's to bury the old lady. Do it."

"But I don't know—"

"You don't know shit. Leave Mama, as they say, to God, and leave me the hell alone."

Father Jack stood up. "I'll wait out front, Texana, unless you'd rather...?"

I smiled up at him reassuringly. "I won't be long." I turned back to Matt. "Did you ever go across to see your mother?"

"I'm a wanted man over there."

"You were seen."

"Shit." His speech moved back and forth from English to Spanish, but the curse was in English. He poured himself a second glass of sotol and drank it. "I tried to borrow money. She didn't have any. She could have made some cash on that curing business, but she wouldn't take money for it. I thought she was crazy, picking weeds and drying them, talking about the old cures the Indians used. Hell, who'd have thought she could cure people. She got real popular." He shook his head in puzzlement. "She said the Bible said that some people are granted gifts of healing by the Spirit."

"And she wouldn't sell God's gift," I said.

Matt nodded, put the bottle to his lips, drank, and said resentfully, "That rancher that bought our land from her—"

"Robert Darke?"

"He offered to start her in business, selling those herbs in health food stores. She told him no."

"Money didn't mean much, then, to your mother?"

"Sure as hell never seemed to. Good thing, considering we never had a pot to piss in. Mama always had the time to cure every bellyache and boil on both sides of the river. Asking for a dollar or two in return might have swelled the huge estate she left me," he said sarcastically. He reached out for one of the packages of cupcakes, tore it open, and bit into one. A mustache of white filling gleamed on his upper lip. He washed the cupcake down with another drink from the bottle.

"Hell, Mama was thirty-two when she had me, thirty-six when Luke come along. I never knew anything about her life before she was my mother. What do I know about her religion or what she believed? She'd never say nothing about the past. I don't even know where she was born. She always said it wasn't good for a person to dwell on the past. She said live today and think about tomorrow and let go of everything else. Fine talk if you've got fucking-all to look forward to."

"Did your mother ever say anything about a witch, someone who gave her the evil eye or put a hex on her?"

"That superstitious crap! Don't tell me you believe in it?"

"I notice your shop sells herbal remedies."

He laughed. "Crap. Like everything else we sell. Lots of chumps out there will buy anything. We sell a floral spray that smells like some pansy room deodorizer and that guarantees on the label to make the buyer irresistible to a lover. I don't have to believe in it to sell it. A poor boy's got to make a living somehow."

"I want to know what your mother believed about the evil eye."

He heaved a disgusted, and disgusting, breath. "Sometime last spring she said she'd had a customer who had an evil eye."

"She said those exact words—'had' an evil eye, not 'gave' the evil eye?"

He shrugged and tipped the bottle again. "Evil eye, walleyed. What difference does it make."

"Did she say if the customer was a man or a woman?"

"No."

"Your mother went to see Doña Aurora for a sweeping because of the evil eye. Did she take any other action?"

He gave me a scornful look. "Like what? How would I know?"

"Did your mother ever say anything to you about one of her clients that she couldn't cure? Someone who might have had a grudge against her?"

"Why? You think somebody figured she was a witch? If I'd thought she could hex people, I'd have had her hex my wife's whole family, especially my wife." He shook his head. "As far as I know, the old lady's cures were one hundred percent successful. Make that ninety-nine. She said I drank too much and she gave me some herb mixture to take that was supposed to stop me drinking. It gave me the trots." He smirked and lifted the bottle to his lips.

"One last thing, then," I said. "Do you know where I can find Luke?"

"No idea." He paused, staring at me. "No idea what-the-hell business it is of yours either," he said, the drug-and-alcohol-induced neutrality evolving into belligerence. "This is a shithole of a country. The politicians are shit, the peso is shit, the life is shit. If the old lady had money, I'd have killed her myself to get out of here. She's dead. I'm here, turning to shit."

I stood. I wanted to get out of there before the effects of the sotol turned him aggressive. As I moved toward the door, he roused himself and got to his feet, waving the bottle in his hand and toppling the table.

"You want to know about my mama's life," he yelled, "ask that cold-assed bitch who was writing a book about her."

"Who? What's her name?"

He lifted the bottle toward his mouth. "Miss Linden Too-Good-To-Talk-To-Trash-Like-Me Fonda. Bitch."

Matt's loud voice brought Father Jack to the doorway. At the sight of the priest, Matt snarled a further epithet and hurled himself forward. I put my hands on the shoulders of the priest, spun him around, and got us out of there. As we passed Matt's startled wife and reached the shop door, I looked back and saw the drunken Matt swaying in the doorway.

"Next time bring whiskey," he shouted at me.

Father Jack and I hit the street at a fast walk and kept going to the corner.

"God Almighty! Is he always like that?" Father Jack asked, huffing along beside me.

"Matt was every teacher's nightmare, a loud-mouth connected to a pea-brain."

"This visit was a bust for me," Father Jack said.

"I still don't know what to do for the old lady. Any suggestions?"

My mind still on Matt Fair, I wasn't able to concentrate on the priest's question. Instead, I suggested we return to a border station by way of Avenida de las Americas, a longer walk but less crowded by pedestrians.

Father Jack responded, "Can't we get a cab? That's a pretty good walk for these priestly legs." He stopped to look over a taco vendor's selection.

Shaking my finger at the greasy morsels, I said, "Better not. Eat one of those and you might be walking a little faster than you want. The walk will do you good."

"What do you mean, Texana? You think the old padre could use the exercise?"

Father Jack's a good sport, so I didn't mind saying, "That knit shirt is taking all the strain it can. You don't want to end up looking like the Michelin man."

He laughed and retorted, "Gee, some of Matt Fair's attitude must have rubbed off on you." He looked down at his portly stomach and rubbed his hand across the stretched knit. "I'm not genuflecting as much as I used to," he sighed.

We continued walking, taking in the upscale boutiques and swank hotels in this section of the city.

"About Mrs. Fair's funeral," I said, returning to the priest's original concern. "She didn't have any money and her sons are worthless. Let's go full-out for her funeral, coffin, Mass, flowers, and headstone. Can't you take up a special collection for a couple of Sundays to pay the expenses?"

Father Jack stopped walking to stare at me. "My parishioners are old ladies in black, mothers with eight children, and a handful of men too old or too hungover to escape coming to Mass with the womenfolk. All of them are too poor to afford a Poor Box. And there's no money in the coffers for a coffin," he noted wryly.

"Well, doesn't the diocese have a special fund to bury the destitute?"

"A free Mass, sure, but you're asking His Grace to shell out big bucks for a casket and all the trimmings. No, I don't think so. Besides, the bishop is making his ad limina visit to Rome right now, and I refuse to prostrate myself before that beastly Monsignor Gomez to beg coins for a freebie funeral."

"So what are you telling me, Father?" I said indignantly. "We've got to do something."

"We'll do as poor Matt suggested and leave it to God. And the county commissioners. A pauper's prayer service need not be undignified."

I shut my mouth before I echoed Matt and said *Shit.* I'd arrange something for Rhea when I got home. In the meantime, I slowed the pace I had been setting and led Father Jack to Julio's Café Corona for an early dinner.

While the priest settled in to enjoy his black bass à la Veracruz, I ate spicy chicken and avocado and thought out my plans. I wouldn't be driving home tonight. I had made up my mind to go and see the one person who might tell me things about Linden Fonda. More and more it seemed the missing young woman might be the key to discovering why Rhea had been killed.

FOURTEEN

MEXICAN BORDER GUARDS rarely stop persons entering Mexico, and reentry to the U.S. is almost as easy. The U.S. customs officer asked Father Jack and me one simple question—"Where were you born?"—and we stepped back into Texas.

In the parking lot, I bid the priest *"Vaya con Dios"* and headed for a downtown travel agency, where I purchased round-trip airline tickets to San Antonio for the following morning. Next stop, the mall for pajamas, toiletries, a carry-on bag, and a change of clothes. By six p.m. I had left the mall and checked into a motel far enough from El Paso International Airport not to be too expensive.

I placed a call to Andalon at his home, asking him for the name and address of Linden Fonda's aunt and requesting that he call the woman and tell her I would like to visit her sometime the next morning. He agreed, saying he would vouch for me to Leigh Tavers.

My second call was to Clay, letting him know my plans.

"Do you think I'm out of line, wanting to speak with this woman?" I asked him.

"You were the last person to see her niece before the girl vanished. I should think she'd be anxious to talk to you."

We finished the conversation with Clay telling me

about his day, spent as Sunday had been, as Tuesday would be, and who knew how many days to come: vaccinating as many animals as possible and trying to persuade whomever would listen that for the duration of the rabies outbreak it would be wise to keep pets indoors or in a secure enclosure. He told me about a rabid bobcat that had clawed its way through a window screen and attacked a teenager who, hearing the noise, had run to investigate. The boy had been bitten several times on his leg but managed to shoot the animal, killing it. I reminded Clay to be careful.

After we disconnected, I watched a Mexican *telenovela,* bathed, and at ten cut off the light. I slept fitfully, disturbed by the shifting noises in the room next door. Maybe the motel was *too* inexpensive.

Early the next morning, dressed in my new clothes, I left my pickup in airport parking and boarded the Southwest Airlines flight to San Antonio.

Twenty minutes after landing, I had rented a car and bought a map of the city. My first stop was for breakfast. While I ate, I read the newspaper, then lingered over a second cup of coffee. Finally it seemed late enough that Linden Fonda's aunt should be dressed and ready for the day. I telephoned her home to ask permission for my visit.

Leigh Tavers cut off my explanation with a statement: "The sheriff told me about you." She rattled off her address and directions and hung up.

Twenty-five minutes later I pulled up in front of her house. She lived in an American dream gone bad, a single-family home in a decaying neighborhood of treeless yards where shirtless males ducked under the hoods of banged-up cars and ceaselessly repaired carburetors.

I locked the rental car and crossed the lawn, stepping over plastic toys spilling over from the next yard, and rang the bell. It was dead, so I knocked loudly.

The woman who opened the peeling door was desperately thin, and her skin had the waxy look of the seriously ill. Andalon had said Leigh Tavers had been in the hospital when her niece disappeared. I decided the hospital stay must have been for treatment of something serious, perhaps terminal.

She gave me an up-and-down look and stepped aside. I entered and hit a waft of stale, fetid air that stopped my breath and my forward momentum until she pressed a hand against my back and instructed me to go straight ahead.

We walked down a gloomy hall with a scarred wood floor and a rug so dirty I could feel the grit through my shoes. She ushered me into the kitchen. Here the smell was almost overwhelming, a combination of the overflow from the gallon garbage pail in the corner and the unwashed dishes piled in the sink. She pulled out a chair at the table littered with more soiled dishes and seated herself.

"Don't just stand there," she snapped.

I sat, but not before I tipped the chair to spill the worst of the crumbs from the seat. I couldn't do anything about the embedded grime.

At least she didn't apologize for the condition of the house, or pretend it was a temporary situation caused by her illness. She leaned her arms on the table, elbowing aside a plate, and got right to the point.

"I told that sheriff friend of yours like I told the local police: Linden was going to pick me up at the hospital and bring me home and stay with me until I got strong enough to cook for myself and drive again. She promised to be there and she never came. Seems like you're the only one taking an interest. Why would that be?"

"I saw your niece the day she arrived in our area. I own the trading post there. She bought gas from me. The woman she was going to see, Rhea Fair, was a friend. I found Rhea's body."

"So you're here. The sheriff said you had some questions. Ask them."

I ceased trying to ease my way in. If she could be blunt, so could I. "Did Linden ever mention Rhea Fair's name to you?"

"Linden called her a healing woman," Tavers said, wrinkling her nose. "Said she used herbs and eggs and such things to cure people of all kinds of stuff."

"How did Linden learn about Rhea's healing practice?"

"She wrote about the woman in her thesis for graduate school. Linden has her master's degree in creative writing from the University of Texas at El Paso," she added with a hint of pride in the dry tones.

So Linden had known Rhea, which meant that Matt might have been telling the truth yesterday when he said Linden had been planning a book about his mother, perhaps an expansion of her thesis. "Had

Linden said anything to you about writing a book about Rhea Fair? Mrs. Fair's son seemed to think Linden might be planning such a book,'' I explained.

She thought about it. ''Linden and me are not as close as we used to be. I raised her after my sister, her mother, died when Linden was ten. Her father paid for her upkeep and her schooling, but never came around otherwise. Must be seven or eight years since he died, too.''

I cleared my throat and asked, ''Would it distress you too much to tell me about the last time you saw your niece?''

''I'm long past distress,'' she said.

I didn't know whether she meant because of Linden's disappearance or because of her own state of health.

''Linden came to see me at the hospital, I think on the twenty-second or twenty-third of October, but I can't be sure because the medication made me so groggy. She said she had to make a short trip out of town, but that she'd be back in time to help check out and drive me home. Doctor told her I'd need help. She promised she'd stay with me. That's the last time I saw her.''

I asked about twenty more questions and found out a few facts. Linden Fonda worked at the daily newspaper as a feature writer. She'd taken a week of vacation time to make her trip. She'd said nothing to anyone about her destination nor mentioned Rhea Fair in connection with the trip. She had few friends, and none her aunt could name. Tavers' greatest grievance seemed to be the inconvenience to herself caused by the disappearance of her niece.

I was beginning to feel nauseated by the smell of the kitchen. I asked what I hoped would be my last question. "Did Linden ever say that she had received a letter from Rhea Fair? Or written one to her?"

She shook her head. "Linden never mentioned any letters. She did show me a picture of Mrs. Fair sitting under a tree with one of those bug-eyed dogs in her lap."

"A Chihuahua?"

"Very penetrating eyes."

"The dog?"

"Of course not. Mrs. Fair."

"Oh, yes. What was I thinking? Must be jet lag."

"From El Paso?"

I felt myself blush. Sometimes the road to Damascus has more potholes than lightning. I'd rushed halfway across Texas to make a fool of myself.

"You want a glass of water?" Tavers asked. I shook my head, silenced by the very thought of drinking from any glass in that kitchen.

I cleared my throat. "I don't suppose it will help," I told her truthfully, "but do you have a copy of Linden's thesis that I might look over?"

She shook her head. "Not me. You can look in Linden's apartment, if you like. She kept an extra key here. I'll get it."

With an effort, she pushed herself up out of the chair and left the room. I could hear her opening drawers and rummaging. After a few moments, she returned, sat down, and slid a key and a slip of paper with an address written on it across the table. She sighed and turned to stare out the kitchen window, which overlooked a drab fenced backyard with a rusty swing set.

She sighed, and I saw a tear slide down her sunken cheek. "I hope you can find Linden," she said in a tone so soft she might have been talking to herself. "*Linden*—I thought it was a silly name when my sister picked it and I told her so. Name the baby something ordinary, I said, but my sister had seen a picture in some book of a linden tree in bloom, big green heart-shaped leaves and yellow flowers, and that's the name she wanted if her baby was a girl."

FIFTEEN

LINDEN FONDA'S apartment was on the ground floor of a large Spanish-style complex in the middle of a cluster of rental developments in the northwest part of the city. I let myself in with the key and discovered that someone had been there before me. The door of the closet in the tiny entry stood open, and scattered across the tile floor were boxes with the lids off and the contents spilled.

I stepped back outside to examine the door. The paint was clean and undamaged and nothing marked the brass plate around the keyhole. The lock was a dead bolt. That began and ended my expertise on breaking and entering, but it appeared that whoever had gotten in had done so just like me, with a key. Could that key have been taken from Linden? Did the search of the apartment have anything to do with Linden's being missing?

I went inside. I examined the front window, leaving the curtains closed, flipped the light switch by the door, stepped over the debris, and surveyed the combination living-dining area. Whatever the intruder had been after, the search couldn't have taken long. The small room was minimally furnished, but the colors in the framed art posters perfectly complemented the painted wicker and bright rugs. Linden had chosen these things with care, making a snug nest for herself in this rented space. Against the far wall stood the single substantial piece of furniture, an office-style work center with hutch and desk with laminate surfaces and a pullout keyboard shelf. Conspiciously missing was a computer or keyboard. The shelves of the hutch had been emptied and the contents dumped on the floor.

Crossing the room, I knelt and sifted through the pile of papers and notebooks. The jumble of typed pages seemed to be stories about people and places in San Antonio, apparently drafts of material written for the newspaper she worked for. I searched for even one page on the borderland or the *curandera* but found nothing. The notebooks held names and interview notes, with one listing future story ideas, but nothing on Rhea Fair.

Among the rest of the contents of the desk, I found few personal items. No checkbook—Linden might have had it with her—but a neat file of canceled checks and bank records. She had modest spending habits and a small savings account. No address book or phone numbers—those might have been on the computer I assumed the searcher had taken. I did find receipts for utilities, and cash payment receipts for clothes and even groceries had been kept. I envisioned Linden living on her modest salary, planning for the future—a larger apartment, perhaps, or a new car—by keeping meticulous records of the tiniest expenditure.

The more I looked at the evidence of the routine of her life, the more I felt disturbed by her continued absence. She did not seem to be a person who would have disappeared deliberately. She was a person who would have planned her absence with the same care that she organized the rest of life. She would have returned to help her aunt. If she could. Something had gone wrong. Something or someone had prevented her from returning.

I peeked into the galley kitchen. Nothing out of place, nothing disturbed. China stacked on the shelves, the dishwasher empty. The countertop was spotless and organized. In one cabinet, cans and boxes lined up in precise rows.

I glanced back at the mess in the living room. Supposing Linden had returned in a hurry to get something... But I couldn't see her tearing through her own things. If she put something away, she'd be able to place her hands on it instantly. Or to tell someone else where to find it. So if the intruder wasn't random, but had something to do with Linden's being missing, then the person had her keys, but not her cooperation. An argument for her being dead.

One room left. The queen-size bed was fat with floral-print pillows. Ceramic figurines lined the high sill of the window. A popular novel with the author's name in bigger type than the title lay open facedown on a bedside table. I picked it up and flipped through the pages, wishfully thinking that I might find some hidden scrap of paper with a clue to Linden's whereabouts. Checked the window. Locked. Then I tried the bathroom. Spotless, like the kitchen. I opened the medicine chest. Even the toothbrush looked new. Aspirin, floss, hair spray. No birth-control pills. But she would have taken those with her, if she used them.

I closed the door of the medicine cabinet and stared at myself in the glass. What was I doing? Mrs. Tavers had given me permission to look in the apart-

ment for a copy of Linden's thesis, not to snoop in
her medicine cabinet. This was a terrible intrusion. I
recalled Leigh Tavers' face as she stared out the window. She was glad someone cared enough to ask
questions. I hoped Linden would forgive my intrusion into her privacy for her aunt's sake. Maybe for
her own sake.

Linden stored her books on brick-and-board
shelves against the one blank wall of the bedroom.
A mix of well-used literature and history books took
up most of the space. She had bought used books, or
perhaps the volumes had belonged to her parents.
Textbooks from her college days stood tightly
packed on the top shelf, along with a fair collection
of paperbacks on folklore of Mexico and the Southwest. A stack of binders filled the corner space.

I took them down. Spreading the notebooks on the
bed, I found they had been kept in order from Linden's freshman year through graduate school. In
beautifully rounded handwriting that changed little
over the five-year span she had recorded meticulous
notes. No doodles. No marking out. No scribbled
personal notes to the student sitting next to her. I had
a sense of a serious, purposeful young woman.

Whatever the notebooks illuminated about Linden's personality, they revealed nothing about her
thesis project on the *curandera*. And no thesis anywhere on the shelves. I ran my finger across the
spines of the books on each shelf to be sure.

Linden had kept her college texts and notebooks.
She would have kept a copy of her thesis. There had
been room on top of the stacked notebooks for a
bound thesis. Had that disappeared, like the com-

puter, with the intruder? But why? And why was there no trace in this apartment of Linden's connection to Rhea Fair?

Walking across the room, I picked up a photograph that stood in a silvery frame on top of the dresser. A smiling Linden Fonda, looking much as she had the day she stopped at the trading post, stared back at me from a color portrait done in Jessica Rex's intriguing style and featuring her *new* technique, which gave a soft, dusky finish to the photo. Jessica had said she was not a professional photographer. How had she come to take this picture? Why had she never mentioned that she knew the missing woman? Gently, I put the photograph down.

I finished what I had come to do—look for the thesis—and now I tried to find what the previous searcher had wanted. I checked the top right-hand drawer of the dresser. Inside were a few neatly folded scarves and a wooden box with an angel painted on the lid. I took it out and opened it. It held jewelry— six pairs of earrings, three gold chains, and a ring that looked like an antique and was set with an opal. If real, the ring was valuable. If the searcher had been simply a burglar, the ring wouldn't have been overlooked. I replaced the box and checked the remaining drawers; the clothing inside was folded and organized. Why hadn't the person who searched the living room torn through these drawers, too? Because there was nothing to be found, and the searcher had known this?

I took the photo in its silver frame and set it on the kitchen counter beside the telephone while I called Mrs. Tavers.

I asked, "Did Linden ever mention someone named Jessica Rex?"

"I don't know the name. Like I told you, Linden kept to herself after she got out on her own. She called regular, but she didn't visit much, or talk about her life."

I told Mrs. Tavers about the photo and asked if I might borrow it. She agreed. Then I told her about the unknown person's search of the apartment.

"A burglary?" she asked.

"The windows are locked and the locks on the doors work. I think whoever it was got in with a key. Did Linden give extra copies to anyone? Maybe a former roommate?"

"She lived alone as far as I know. Privacy was real important to her. Always kept the door to her room closed when she was a kid." She paused. "When I reported her missing, the police got the apartment manager to let them in. They didn't find anything out of place."

"I think you should call them and report this."

"You say the doors and windows are okay. If it's not a break-in, those police won't bother."

I pressed the point.

"I called them when she went missing," she said, sounding exasperated. "She was an adult, they said, and had a right to be away without telling anybody. They thought she was off with some boyfriend. Linden feels things deep, I told them. She wouldn't just go off with somebody for a fling. I could see by their faces they thought I was foolish. I call now, and they'll think she came back for her computer. Maybe she did. I don't know what to think." She sighed deeply, and I could hear the exhaustion in her voice. Leigh Tavers' illness had drained her of the stamina to fight a bureaucratic mind-set, even for the sake of her niece.

"Besides," she added, "what can the police do here? Linden disappeared out where you live. You find her for me, you and that sheriff friend of yours. You find Linden."

What could I say? I told her I would try. I offered to drop the key to the apartment by her house, but she told me to leave it there. I said good-bye and put the key down on Linden Fonda's spotless counter. I thought about calling the police myself, but in the face of Mrs. Tavers' wish not to, decided against it.

From the entry, I gave the living room one last look, fixed the lock, and left.

SIXTEEN

I REALIZED once again how much my sense of self depends on my sense of place. Boarding my afternoon return flight in San Antonio, I had wondered what I thought I was playing at, questioning Leigh Tavers, going to Linden Fonda's apartment. But back in the desert city of El Paso and behind the wheel of my own pickup, I felt a resurgence of confidence in the wisdom of my pursuit of information about Linden.

During the flight, as I stared out the plane window and watched the cities thin and the open space assume dominance, I decided to finish what I had started. I would go to the source to see a copy of Linden Fonda's thesis, the university where she had earned her degree.

The University of Texas at El Paso is tucked into the lower rimrock of the Franklin Mountains where the range tips toward and almost touches Mexico. The site, rising with the slope of the mountain range, makes the Bhutanese architecture of the original buildings seem fittingly southwestern.

In the parking area nearest the six-story library, I pulled into a white-lined space marked RESERVED, taking a chance on a ticket from the campus cops in order to save time. The library was located on the southwestern part of the campus overlooking the river. From the the entrance, I paused briefly to look across at the cardboard-and-scrap *colonias* of Juarez where they baked against the barren white earth. What, I wondered, did the residents there, looking toward this side, make of the massive slant-sided buildings rising up from green lawns?

Inside the majestic library, I went past the main counter and directly to the librarian seated at a wide desk cluttered with books and papers. To one side, the screen of the computer terminal glowed, showing a menu. The librarian sat with her hands folded on the desk, staring ahead. She was a plump redhead, and the expression on her face said either it had been a long day or was going to be a long evening.

She jerked herself back to reality as I stopped in front of her desk. She looked up. "How may I help you?"

"Oh, yes. We keep copies of the theses of graduate students," she said when I had explained what I was looking for. She swiveled her chair to face the computer screen. "Do you know the name and the department?"

I spelled the name for her and stated that Linden Fonda's degree was in creative writing.

"Department of English," she said, punching in the information. We waited. Presently several lines of data came up on the screen. The librarian jotted the catalog reference on a slip of paper. "Would you rather look at the shelved copy or the microfiche?" she asked.

"I think I'd like to see the printed copy."

"That's on the fourth floor," she said. She handed me the paper.

I went upstairs and promptly lost all sense of direction as I passed down aisle after aisle until I located the right shelves. I checked the reference on the slip of paper against those marked on the spines of the books, scanning the rows of slim bound volumes to locate the spot where Linden's thesis should have been. It wasn't there. I spent several more minutes trying to find it before giving up. I went back downstairs.

"The computer shows it as available," the librarian said, after I had explained. "Someone might be using it in the library, but it may have been misplaced on the shelves. Let me see if I can find it for you." We went upstairs together to the spot where I had looked, and she trailed her finger down the spines of the documents. "It should be right here." She adjusted her glasses and frowned. Her finger tapped the point where two volumes met while her eyes searched the shelf above and below. "I guess you'll have to use the microfiche copy."

We returned to the reference section and I waited by the microfiche readers while she went to get the film. In a few minutes, she was back, looking embarrassed and apologetic. "I don't understand it," she said. "The microfiche with that thesis is missing."

"Maybe someone is using it," I said.

"I'll see."

I watched while she questioned the only two students using the microfiche readers. She came back shaking her head.

"There should be another copy of the thesis in the special collection on the sixth floor," the librarian told me. "It's not for public use, but under the circumstances I'll ask if we can make an exception."

Back at her desk, I listened as she telephoned someone and explained the situation.

"You may go up," she told me, hanging up the phone.

At the sixth floor, where rare books and collected papers were locked away like gold, I found a competent-looking woman waiting for me.

Smiling, she introduced herself as Janet Saye, librarian for the special collection. "I just retrieved this box of Dr. Winstead's papers. Linden Fonda was one of his students. I recognized the name because she did original research for her paper, and Dr. Winstead was very pleased with her work. I was cataloging his papers at the time and I remember that he encouraged her to stay on for a doctoral degree."

"She wasn't interested?"

"I seem to recall that she was very anxious to get a job and start earning some money. Dr. Winstead kept copies of certain of his students's papers along with his own published works. There should be an extra copy of the thesis you want in here somewhere."

She removed the lid from a deep box marked ORIGINAL RESEARCH: STUDENT, lifted out several bound volumes, and handed me a green-spined thesis. My hand trembled as I read the title typed on a label on the cover: *Rhea Fair: The Story of a Healing Woman.*

"It may not be taken from this room," Janet instructed me. "You may take written notes only. No copies of the text are permitted. I have to stay with you while you read it, since you aren't one of our listed researchers.''

I settled at a table near the librarian's desk and opened the thesis, skipping over the title and other introductory pages to read the body of the typewritten text. There was an explanation of *curanderismo* as a healing art with origins in the Aztec culture. I flipped more pages until I came to what I was most interested in.

Rhea Fair was described as a *curandera* unusually successful in treating physician-diagnosed illnesses, using herbal and psychic cures. I thought of old Trinidad lying in his bed, believing he was being healed by Rhea Fair's psychic energy directed at his pancreas. Linden had given no names or dates of specific cures but had the case histories of clients, the term she used for the *curandera's* patients. Among them, a woman cured of despondency and chronic fatigue, a man cured of a bowel sickness, a child cured of the evil eye that had caused him to weep incessantly, and so on. The story had been written with an eye for colorful image and a feel for the dynamic of emotion working between patient and healer.

I flipped more pages, read descriptions of the plants Rhea gathered and how she utilized them. Flipped more pages, read Linden's brief history of Rhea Fair's knowledge of healing, beginning with her collecting herbs along the border and including her study of herbal *remedios* with a Mexican woman renowned for healing. Linden mentioned Rhea's poverty and her disinclination to use the gift of healing for profit. Nothing on Rhea's personal life or history, except that Linden noted Rhea's lack of formal education and training. She had left school at fifteen and worked at a variety of menial jobs. One quotation from Rhea caught my attention. It was part of a paragraph on the misuse of people's trust by some *curanderos*.

I read a few more pages, came to the lengthy bibliography, and, feeling disappointed, closed the thesis.

"Not finding what you hoped for?"

I looked up to see the librarian staring across at me. "I'm afraid not," I said. I was thinking about Rhea, about the years of poverty and desperation that had driven her, about the healing power she believed had saved her, if not from poverty, then from despair.

"I notice you haven't looked at the material in the back envelope. Maybe those will be what you want."

I must have looked as blank as I felt. She explained that additional documentation for the printed text was in a page-size envelope inside the back cover.

I opened the thesis to the back cover, lifted the thick flap of the manuscript-size envelope, and emptied the contents onto the table.

I unfolded a map showing the border country from El Paso to Presidio, with the ranch road marked to Rhea's line shack and beyond to the Darke Ranch and eventually the interstate. Other documents were the original statements taken from the clients Rhea had treated and whose cures Linden had included in the body of her thesis.

Inside a separate smaller envelope I found several dozen photos of herb plants growing somewhere in the desert, identified by name and a code number on the back that corresponded to notations in the text. Several pictures of Rhea Fair with clients, apparently. A picture of Rhea Fair, scarf tied around her head, a fragile smile on her face, her eyes downcast, standing next to the author of the thesis. Linden looked more at ease than the *curandera*. And younger than she did in the color portrait I had found in her bedroom. In her college days, she had worn her hair longer, and it gave her a childish look.

I held the photograph of the two women and looked closely, trying to read in their faces whatever it was that had tied them together and resulted in the death of one, perhaps both. Two women. And who was the third person present? The person who had taken the photograph. I turned the print over, but the back was blank.

I flipped back to the acknowledgments page of the thesis and found it. Typed last on the list. Photographs: J. Rex.

I made a little noise of surprise in my throat. The librarian glanced up and smiled.

"Find what you're looking for?" she asked.

"Something I wasn't looking for," I told her.

I asked her if I could copy the photo. She offered to do it for me. While she used the copy machine, I thought about Linden Fonda and Jessica Rex. Old friends. Since Linden's college days. Rhea, Linden, Jessica. Was this overlapping of their lives mere coincidence? As far as I knew, Jessica had never mentioned knowing the missing woman. Somewhere there had to be an explanation. I intended to find it.

The hot meal I had promised myself turned into a

fast-food burger and fries. With a Thermos full of hot coffee on the dash, I put the gold-lined clouds of sunset behind me as I drove into the desert toward home.

SEVENTEEN

FIESTA. The day of the rabies vaccinations had begun. Our preparations had been going on for three days. Joe Quiroz had organized the roundup of kid goats and had planned to supervise the cooking, but on Thursday his father had slipped into a diabetic coma and died. Would Rhea Fair's healing have saved Trinidad, I wondered? Certainly the old man had believed so. What part had the resulting psychological distress played in Trinidad's rapid decline? Another death to lay at the feet of Rhea's killer?

With Joe in mourning, Claudia and Ruben Reyes had taken over the barbecuing, making it necessary to shift to my kitchen to prepare the beans, tortillas, and potato salad. It took every platter, plate, and pot I owned. I only just managed to rescue my coffee mug from ending up on the table we had set up in the shade of the post office's cottonwood trees.

Annie Luna and I stood at one of those tables wrapping plastic forks, knives, and spoons in paper napkins.

"Not there! Not there!" I heard Clay shout.

I turned around and saw Clay waving his arms at Charlie and a couple of cowboys as they unloaded the portable toilets Robert Drake's generosity had provided.

"Why in thunder are you putting those so close to the chuck box," Clay yelled. "Put 'em down there."

He pointed toward the far end of town, well past the dining and dancing areas we had marked off with whitewashed rocks.

Charlie laughed, his good nature undeterred by Clay's bad temper. "You better keep them in sight," he told Clay. "Somebody might fancy having one of these modern conveniences and load one up to take home."

Clay shook his head and went back to setting up everything he would need for the vaccinations. Charlie and his helpers manhandled the toilets back onto the pickup and drove farther down the road.

I checked my watch. Noon. Two hours until the official start of the party.

"Quit worrying," said Annie, reading my thoughts. "We'll have a big turnout. Joe and his family did a terrific job of spreading the word."

I forced a smile, my apprehension undiminished by Annie's optimism. Clay was twice as worried as I, unsure whether the threat of rabies was enough to bring the locals and villagers from across the river. Already, Clay had tallied eighteen cases of rabies in dogs and coyotes, plus one bobcat and three foxes. A toddler bitten by one of the foxes was the latest to undergo shots. But it was the virulent strain that had jumped from dogs to coyotes that worried Clay the most. Coyotes, wily, fast, and wide-ranging in their territories, posed the greatest threat to humans through bites to pets and livestock. Word had been passed, as Annie had said, and we could only wait and hope.

Annie paused in wrapping utensils and laughed.

"Look at that," she said, nudging me with her elbow.

I looked up and saw Glafiro Paredes's ancient pickup, front end hoisted behind a massive tow truck. The Letter Man himself rode in state behind the wheel of his beloved but undependable vehicle. The sight lifted my spirits. Glafiro had been bitten by White Dog, was undergoing rabies treatment, and remained healthy. The people on the other side knew and trusted him. Perhaps his example would convince them of the seriousness of the situation and win their cooperation.

"Who's driving the tow truck?" I asked Annie.

"That's one of Lucy's nephews," she said. "I forget his name. He works out of Presidio, mostly towing RVs that break down in our high summer temperatures or get into trouble because of the grade of the river road."

The Letter Man's arrival had started the dogs barking and the younger children—the new teacher had let school out early—shouting and laughing. I could smell the *cabrito,* and my mouth watered. Someone cut on a boom box and Tejano music vibrated the air. An hour later, the arrival of four generations of the prolific Rosales family in their open cattle trailer pulled by an antique John Deere tractor signaled the opening of the fiesta. The Rosaleses were always the first to arrive and the last to leave any celebration.

No sooner had Annie and I wrapped the last napkin around the last three utensils than a stream of old vehicles began arriving from across the river, the drivers double-and triple-parking where they pleased and unloading occupants, human and animal, in large numbers. Several enterprising souls had utilized old ranch gates to convert the beds of their pickups into livestock trailers.

Clay, standing on a makeshift platform of crates, welcomed everyone and invited the people to help themselves to the food while their animals were attended to, pointing out the pens set up as holding areas for pets and livestock. As his crew of volunteers began unloading, sorting, and checking animals, Clay joked to the crowd, "When you head home, please don't leave any of your critters in town. We've already got enough strays to keep us in Christmas tamales for years to come."

I dished food, poured tea, served beer, mopped up, served more food. The tables filled, and the overflow moved onto Lucy's porch and into the road. Some people ate standing up, using tailgates as tables. Doña Aurora did a brisk business in fortune-telling. The brass band played loud and fast, if not melodiously; no one seemed to mind. At last, when the request for refills slowed and the band changed its tune to dance numbers, Annie and Claudia and I took a break.

Feeling a headache lurking behind my eyes, I left the others to their late meal and walked away from the noise and laughter toward the relative quiet of the riverbank. It was nearly five, and the late afternoon sun burned the pavement of the road and the sand of the bank, but the long shadows of the trees at the river's edge created an uneven line of cooling shade where the wiser drivers had parked their vehicles. I found a pickup with the tailgate lowered that offered a seat in the shade and quiet I needed. I sat

on the tailgate. There was a cooler filled with the
super-sweet soft drinks made in Mexico. I lifted out
a chunk of ice and rubbed it across my forehead. It
felt blissfully cooling.

"Next thing," said a lazy voice from the cab of
the pickup, "you'll be pilfering one of my friend
Efrain's sodas, Texsee."

I recognized both the voice and the irritating nick-
name. No matter how many times during our school-
days I told Luke "My name is Texana," he'd always
called me Texsee. Rhea Fair's youngest child had
come home.

I looked over my shoulder as Luke emerged from
the pickup. He gave a quick glance around as if fearful of who might be watching and ambled back in
his long-legged walk to stand beside the tailgate.

"Luke, I'm glad to see you," I said. "I'm really
sorry about your mother."

Skinny as a bamboo pole, he gave me a half-smile
from under a crushed and stained straw cowboy hat
bandaged with silver duct tape to keep crown and
brim married. A polyester shirt, frayed jeans, and red
tennis shoes pegged Luke at the lower end of western
fashion.

"You come over to the trading post," I told him,
"and I'll set you up with a new hat for your mother's
funeral."

"This is my lucky hat," he said as he took it off
and held it up for reverencing. "I was thumbing on
385 when some teenagers in a Mercedes tossed this
out the window at me." He twirled the hat on his
finger. "I was burning up under the noonday sun,

and I blessed those spirited scamps. It's served me well, this old hat." He plunked it back on his head.

"And the luck?"

"Some toothless farmer give me a lift soon afterwards. Few miles down the road, we see the Mercedes hemmed in by two highway patrol cars and a county mountie. Even a game warden was in on the bust. Those kids was prone on the ground with the wet nose of one of them drug-sniffing dogs prowling their designer-clad crotches. If I'd been on board, guess who'd be cooling his heels in the county jail? Like I say, this here's my lucky hat."

Luke laughed at his own tale, then ducked his head and looked shifty-eyed. "Is the law around?" he asked.

"Not to worry. Andalon had other business today. And our constable's busy dancing with Annie Luna. Will you stay over here for the funeral?"

He cleared his throat and seemed to have trouble getting his words out. "Yeah. I got word it was tomorrow. Been living in Chihuahua with some friends. Should have waited until tomorrow, I reckon, to cross over, but I get mighty lonesome for this side of the river sometimes. A fiesta seemed safe enough. It's been a few years since anybody over here seen me. I figured I'd aged enough to look different."

I refrained from saying what I thought: that no one on this side much cared whether or not Luke was back, or gave any thought to turning him in, if he was recognized. Luke was old news. Instead, I mentioned that I'd seen Matt.

"How's he looking?" Luke asked. Much in his tone, but no concern.

"I think he must have let his subscription to *Gentleman's Quarterly* lapse. He lives in the back of a curio shop that his wife runs while he drinks too much sotol."

Luke digested this a while without comment.

"Remember the time," he said, "Matt got liquored up and took an ax and cut down the main electric power pole in El Polvo and blew the substation transformer?"

"All hell broke loose," I said, smiling at the memory. "Half the town hit the street and fired guns in the air. Dogs barking everywhere, babies crying—"

"And Nestor Mooney thought he'd calm the citizenry down by turning on the lights and siren on the volunteer fire truck and driving it up and down yelling, 'Don't panic! I'm in control!'"

"Except he wasn't," I said. "He ran over two of Pete Rosales's dogs."

Luke threw back his head and laughed. "And them Rosales kids chased after the fire truck and pelted Nestor with rocks 'til he finally found the right gear and outdistanced them."

Still chuckling at the memory, Luke dug in the cooler and pulled out a dripping bottle of beer. He used the under edge of the bumper for an opener and perched on the tailgate beside me.

"Olcott Pyne, he was sheriff then, remember?" he said. "Pyne found Matt, in a Future Farmers of America jacket that he'd stole, sitting by that downed pole, whiskey bottle in hand, singing the high school fight song."

"Didn't Pyne handcuff Matt to the front of his

pickup while they waited for the crew from the electric co-op to arrive?''

Luke was using his thumb to peel the label of the beer bottle. ''Yeah, that was Matt's first real arrest. Before that everybody sort of looked the other way 'cause he was a kid and might grow out of it.''

''And because everyone liked your mother,'' I added, remembering Rhea's pleading looks and words with the teachers Matt defied, merchants he shoplifted from, landowners whose property he had damaged, and, in his teenage years, fathers whose daughters he had kept out all night. From his youngest days, Matt had always been in trouble, and on both sides of the border.

''Mama tried to pray us out of the hell we was making for ourselves,'' Luke said. ''When we was young, she'd make us copy scripture verses over and over on strips of Red Chief tablets. She'd hand out them verses to the folks across the river. She checked to make sure we was copying them exactly right, but Matt slipped one by her one time. He wrote: 'No servant is greater than his master, no messenger is greater than the one who sent him, and no fucker leaves this life alive.' The priest found that copy under a lighted candle in the church, recognized the source, and brought it to Mama. She was so mad, Matt hid out for a week across the river at Johnny Chavez's house.''

''I remember when the border patrol would come to school, Johnny Chavez would run for the river and Matt would run with him,'' I said.

Luke swallowed the last drop of his beer and

tossed the bottle over his shoulder. It hit the bed of the pickup with a thud but didn't break.

"Matt and Johnny thought alike. Humming with criminal mischief, somebody said. It was Johnny gave Matt his first taste of smuggling. Old Man Chavez supported all them kids by his smuggling everything from TVs to Christmas lights into Mexico, and Johnny followed in his daddy's footsteps."

"Why Christmas lights?"

He shot me an astonished look. "Hell, Texsee, you've lived your whole life on the border and you don't know? The whorehouses string 'em up as advertising, and it's hard to find 'em in Mexico—the lights, I mean. You might say Old Man Chavez raised his kids on the spirit of Christmas."

He grinned broadly and nudged me with a bony elbow.

I thought about Connie Chavez, Matt's wife, and the dismal shop where Father Jack and I had found Matt. I seemed to recall several strands of Christmas lights hanging around the doorway and dangling above the windows. Apparently Mr. Chavez's daughter sold more Christmas spirit than curios.

Luke slipped off the tailgate. "I can't stand the smell of them pork rinds frying no more. I got to get me some. Come on, Texsee. My treat."

I followed him the few hundred feet across the road to where one entrepreneur had dug his fire pit and was busy dropping pork rinds into fat sizzling in a grease-blackened skillet. As soon as they were crisp, the old man lifted them out of the skillet and popped them into a folded piece of newspaper. The *chicharrones* sold as fast as he could cook them.

Luke paid for three portions, handing one to me. We carried the oily bundles back toward the pickup. I had been too busy and too squeamish to eat the barbecue—the kid goat I'd bought last week had been part of my contribution. I know that all meat comes from some poor animal, but I draw the line at eating one I've looked in the eye.

We resumed our perches on the tailgate. Luke fished out two more beers and passed one to me. Iced beer and hot pork rinds are heaven, and for some time the only sounds were munching and chugging. My mind wasn't idle, though. I had spent too much time since the San Antonio trip trying to put together the events surrounding the *curandera's* murder. Like the frequent mirages that can shift reality in the desert, I had shifted my perspectives on the reality of who might have murdered Rhea Fair, but I still had only suspicions. Guesses, really. My mind chased phantom suspects. I had yet to discover a motive. Without concrete evidence, I could offer no suggestion that was any better than Andalon's belief that drug smugglers had killed the *curandera*. Luke was my last chance to find an answer to Rhea's death in the details of her life. With Luke in a reminiscent mood, perhaps he'd give me the fact that I needed if I let him talk himself out. If not, after he felt more at ease being on this side of the river again, I'd question him about his mother's relationship with Linden Fonda and ask him what he could tell me about Jessica Rex.

Luke finished his last pork rind, wadded up the greasy sheet of newspaper, and threw it behind him to join the spent beer bottles.

"About Matt," I said, intending to bring his reminiscing up to recent events. But his mind was still on his nemesis, Johnny Chavez.

"It was Johnny that was supposed to be riding with Matt in the cattle trailer," he said, scratching the back of his neck. "Johnny got bored with small-time smuggling and got a little too cute for his own good. He built a cattle trailer with a false bottom for drugs. He thought no lawman would want to unload sixteen head of agitated Brahmans and shovel cow shit to check the trailer frame. Johnny paid Matt to go along as the second driver. The first trip was a breeze. A bribe to Mexican customs, and from there on it was an easy trip to San Angelo, where the transfer was made for hauling the product to the waiting junkies in Dallas. Chavez made a ton of money, and the cattle got to see a lot of country and return home with their heads still connected to their spines."

"I guess the success soon ended," I said, prodding him to get to the climax.

He nodded, frowning. "The second trip, Chavez couldn't go. Matt needed a second driver to spell him, so I went along. Sheriff Pyne pulled us over just outside Shafter, just to hassle us, we thought. As soon as we stopped and stepped out of the truck, out come the DEA agents from one of the old adobe buildings. They unloaded the cattle at the loading pens on the Circle J. The agent let Sheriff Pyne do the honors of lifting out the first floorboard. It didn't take that bandy-legged aggravation no time at all to find our tickets to the penitentiary. By nightfall, we was in jail and Matt had made his call to Mama, begging her to find us a lawyer.

"Mama didn't have no money," he continued, "and nobody would take us as clients, so the court appointed some pink-fingered kid right out of law school. Sheriff Pyne hooted at that, said he could see we had a forceful legal talent on our side. Matt said we was done for."

I swatted at a fly buzzing around the damp lip of my bottle of beer. Across the river, a lone buzzard circled tirelessly in the empty sky.

Luke sighed deeply and said, "Me and Matt, we never saw a badge we didn't think we could best, but we never figured on getting caught by the Feds. We was scared shitless. When our bail was set, it was so high no bondsman would touch it, not with us so close to Mexico and plenty of friends on the other side. I never saw Mama so upset. She told me she knew someone she could call on for help if she had to—"

"Here you are."

I looked up to see Father Jack striding toward us. He carried an overloaded plate of barbecue in one hand and two bottles of beer in the other. When he got close enough to touch, he stopped, beaming at me and glancing curiously at Luke.

"Clay's looking for you, Texana," he announced. "We've blessed and vaccinated everything with four legs. Now we can eat. Clay fixed a plate for you, too."

Listening to Luke, I'd forgotten about the fiesta and its purpose. I introduced him to the priest, who, between bites of food, explained the plans for Rhea's funeral.

"We thought a plain and simple graveside service

best,'' he summed up, having glossed over the stinginess of the details.

Luke looked at his feet, then at Father Jack. He slid off the tailgate and walked a short distance away from us, then turned and said, ''Whatever you got planned is what'll be done. Thanks.''

He hesitated, then added, ''Matt and me caused Mama some bad days. Rebellion, that's what it was. But against what I don't know. We loved Mama. Daddy spent most of his time doctoring wormy cows, but we missed him when he died, and we loved Mama even more. She always saw to it we was clothed, fed, housed, and loved, not high on the hill, but better than lots of folks around here.''

His guilt is getting the better of him, I thought.

''There'll be a lot of flowers for your mother,'' I told him, ''from both sides of the river. Rhea was well thought of around here.''

Father Jack nodded, patted me on the shoulder—presumably because he was too lazy to walk over and pat Luke—and left us.

Luke came back to the tailgate, but remained standing this time.

''Mama had a hard life,'' he said.

''She never complained. She never held losing the ranch against you or Matt. She'd like it if you were at the funeral. I don't suppose Matt will be here.''

He shook his head. ''No, not Matt. Didn't have much time for her when she was alive.'' There was anger in his voice and on his face. I hadn't expected that. As a kid, Luke had idolized his big brother, always following Matt's dubious lead.

He tilted his head and looked at me. "You reckon Andalon will be at the funeral?"

I shook my head. "I imagine he expects you to be here, and if he came, he'd have to arrest you. I don't think he wants to do that."

He nodded, then started down memory lane again. "Remember—"

I had to interrupt if I wanted to move him past 1975. "Do you know a woman named Linden Fonda?"

"Nope. Wait a minute. Yes, I do. She wrote some story or other about Mama, must have been three or four years ago. Matt met her and tried some moves on her." He chuckled. "She shot him down fast."

"Did your mother ever talk about her?"

"Not to me. I only seen Mama two or three times since Matt and me took off to Mexico."

"Did you ever hear your mother mention a Jessica Rex?"

Luke shifted restlessly from one foot to the other. His eyes focused on some point above my head. He'd had too many run-ins with the law to enjoy being questioned, even by his old friend Texsee.

"I never heard no such name," he finally answered. "Mama could keep a tight lip."

And had to, with two such reprobate sons, I thought.

"Only one more question," I told him. He gave me a sharp look, unmollified. It wouldn't have surprised me if he ran for the river, like Matt in the old days.

"Never mind, Luke," I said. "I don't know what

else to ask." I stood up, extended a hand to him, and bid him good-bye.

"See you tomorrow then, Texsee," he said, suddenly more cheerful. "If you see Efrain, tell him I'll meet him on the other side. He'll know where."

I slipped off the tailgate and started toward the other end of town. I'd walked about fifty feet before I realized I did have another question. I shouted, "Wait up, Luke," and trotted after him.

I caught up to him and asked, "When you needed bail money you said your mother told you there was someone she could ask for help. Did she mean financial help?"

"I guess. Sure was what we needed."

"Who was she talking about? Was it Robert Darke?"

"Darke?" He gave me a puzzled look. "No. She was talking about her first husband. But she never called him, I don't guess, since she put the ranch up for our bail."

"Her first husband?" I repeated stupidly. I had been so sure I had a connection to Robert Darke, who seemed to loom in the background of Rhea's life, buying her ranch when she had to sell, offering to market her herbal remedies, recommending her curative powers to his pet archaeologist.

"And before you ask," Luke said, "I don't know his name nor nothing about him. When I was maybe nine or ten, I found a picture in Mama's keepsake box and asked her about it. Mama told me it was her and a school friend and snatched it out of my hand. Afterwards she hid that keepsake box away and I never saw it no more until she moved to the line shack. I used to see it there when I sneaked across to visit.''

"How did you know it was your mother's first husband in the picture?''

"I asked her. I saw that box and remembered the picture, and I asked her who the fellow was. She told me and said he was the one she thought about asking for help, but she decided not to. 'Past is past,' she said, 'and you ought not to go reclaiming it.' Never named the fellow nor said anything about when they married, except to say they was real young. 'He helped me to get away from home, and we parted friends,' she said. Mama was real pretty in that picture,'' Luke added softly. He looked at me, puzzled. "Is any of this important?''

"I don't know,'' I told him.

"I'll see you tomorrow,'' he said, turning away and starting down the sandy bank, half walking, half sliding.

EIGHTEEN

CLAY AND BILLY DEED sat eating a much-delayed meal at a table littered with soiled paper plates and empty drink bottles. Around them, activity swirled as mothers herded darting children and young men lolled against pickups and gave slick-eyed looks at young women watching them right back. In the shade, the old people fanned their faces and gossiped in low voices.

As I approached, Clay pushed aside his plate, reached for his glass of tea, and smiled. I sat down beside him.

"I ate your plate of food and mine," he said. He refilled his glass of tea, leaned back in his chair, and crossed his arms over his stomach.

"I've eaten. You look tired, but pleased," I said to him.

"Billy tallied the turnout at close to three hundred and fifty people," Clay said in a satisfied voice.

"Give or take a Rosales or two," Billy said. "Everything went great. Only two serious drunks, no fights, no gunfire, and I sent the boys with the fighting cocks back across the river to do their betting."

I smiled at Billy's enthusiasm and turned to look at Clay. "And the vaccinations?" I asked him.

He smiled broadly. "Any more customers and I'd have run out of vaccine. Now, when the coyotes start their sunset howling, I'll worry a little less."

A man and boy driving a herd of goats, their bells clanging and tinkling, waved at us as they aimed the docile animals toward the river.

"Did you send Father Jack looking for me?" I asked Clay.

Billy laughed. My husband looked sheepish.

"I may have given him the idea it would be a big help if he could find you," Clay admitted.

"He wanted him out of his hair," Billy said grinning. He nudged Clay's shoulder. "I heard Father Jack lecturing you about how deprived we are here on the border. He also cornered the whole Rosales clan and tried to persuade them to join his goat-cheese cooperative."

"The Rosales family is big enough to form a co-operative on their own. Pete wasn't interested, was he?" I said.

"Not a bit." Billy said. "How many priests have we had?"

"Three in eight years," I said.

"Jack will get tired of trying to change us and request a transfer," Clay said. "Right now, he's still feeling the zeal of needing to save us from our cultural and economic deprivation, as he puts it."

"I call it peace and quiet," I said.

"Amen," said Billy, rising. "Speaking of which, I'd better walk around and make sure everything is still peaceful. I'll come back and help you with the cleanup, Texana."

I nodded and smiled, knowing that his offer to help was because he knew Annie would be helping me.

"He's intelligent, handsome, and well mannered,"

I said to Clay as we watched Billy go. "What more could Annie want?"

"Don't go promoting that romance. Annie will never marry him."

"You don't know that."

"Annie is bored sick here, and Billy is an antidote. Also, he's just black enough and Protestant enough to irritate her father, which at the moment it pleases her to do."

"Annie mistakes her resentment of her family as hatred for the border, that's all. She'll mature, like I did, and realize that this is home."

Clay put his arm across my shoulder and gave me a hug. "Not everybody, Dorothy, wants to click their heels together and go back to Kansas."

Before I could make a retort, he changed the subject by asking how my day had gone.

"I had a conversation with Luke Fair."

He sat up. "Did you now?"

I nodded. "He's feeling guilty about his mother's death. Luke always made promises he couldn't keep, especially to himself. I imagined he'd been daydreaming of coming up lucky, making a lot of easy money, and buying back the ranch for his mother."

"Sounds like he believes more in luck than hard work," said Clay.

"The Fair men all believed in luck. They just never had any."

Clay rocked his chair back, crossed his arms over his chest, and said, "Well, what did he have to say?"

"Luke told me something about Rhea, though I can't say it helps in finding her killer." I told Clay about Rhea's being married before she met Jake Fair.

"Maybe Luke's worried he's a bastard," Clay said.

"Born and not made, you mean?"

He ignored my sarcasm. "You've been uncommonly quiet since you got back from El Paso. Worrying over something?"

"Why is it you always think I have to be either sick or worried to be quiet?"

"There's no safe way for me to answer that," he hedged, "so talk. What did you find out in San Antonio?"

"I've hardly seen you the past three days, and when I have, you've been exhausted. I've waited to discuss it with you until this fiesta business was over and you had time to relax."

He stretched his arms wide. "I'm relaxed."

I told him in detail about my conversation with Leigh Tavers, the search of Linden's apartment, and what I found at the university.

"This photograph, the one from the apartment," Clay said. "You're sure she took it?"

"It looks like a Jessica Rex to me. I'll show it to you when we get home and you can judge for yourself."

A parade of pickups and cars moved in a slow, erratic line toward the river. Last in line came the Rosales's tractor pulling the trailer crammed with squealing children and bawling goats. Fiesta had ended.

"Here's what I think," I said. "Someone had Linden's key and searched her apartment to remove any evidence of a connection between the *curandera* and Linden."

"Possibly," Clay said.

"Beyond that, I have no answers."

"And the connection between Linden and Jessica?"

"I don't know where to go with that. I can hardly ask Jessica. It's none of my business, and she'd have no reason to give me an answer."

"You might mention it to Andalon," Clay said.

"Oh, yeah. He already thinks he's indulged me by arranging for me to see Mrs. Tavers. I will tell him, though. When I talk to him. It isn't like he called to ask me what Mrs. Tavers had to say, or if I found out anything."

"Do you think you did find anything significant?"

I shook my head. "For the past two days I've been speculating about who might have murdered the *curandera*. I can't fit anyone we know into the mold of a killer. Unless Andalon is right about her murder, the answer has to be with Rhea's life, but where? Who felt threatened by her, or why? No one stood to gain by her death. She had no money. She didn't even seem interested in making money. If she had, she'd have accepted Robert's offer to market her herbal cures."

"If Rhea didn't want money," Clay said, "most people do. Maybe she stood in someone's way."

"Matt wants money desperately to get out of Mexico and away from his wife, but his mother's death doesn't benefit him."

"If you're stuck on first base, the only place to try for is second base." Clay cocked his head and looked at me. "What's your next step?"

Until he asked, I hadn't known.

"Ask Billy to let me go through his mother's things. Maybe I'll find something that will explain what Rhea was so worried about last spring that she went to Maria for advice."

Clay pushed his chair back and stood up. "I'll help Annie with the cleanup. You go and find Billy." He began to collect the paper trash.

Nearby, Ruben was tossing water over the coals where the *cabrito* had cooked. A group of children made a game of carrying off the whitewashed rocks and piling them behind the post office. The band had packed up and departed. Most of the residents of El Polvo picked up trash, carried tables and chairs back home, sorted dishes, and generally restored order.

I spied Billy laughing with Annie and heartlessly interrupted them.

NINETEEN

THE DAY of the funeral, I closed the trading post. Normally, I do this only on Christmas and Easter, and even on those high holy days locals know to knock at the back door in case of emergency.

The Mass bell tolled at ten o'clock. On border time, this meant the mourners were making their way inside the church by twenty minutes after ten. It was to be a double funeral.

When Joe Quiroz had learned that Rhea's funeral had been scheduled for the same day, different hour, as the Mass for his father, he had suggested a joint service for the two old friends. Father Jack had readily agreed.

Of the large number of mourners, the turnout from the other side amazed me. Our small church accommodates fifty people. Today the crowd flowed out the door, waiting patiently in line to file past the caskets and pay their respects to the dead.

Rhea's willow-wood casket had been draped with a bright fringed shawl, which I recognized as belonging to Doña Aurora. A framed photograph resting in the center of the casket showed a youthful Rhea smiling into the camera beside her husband, Jake. I wondered if Luke had supplied it. Around the photo, someone had placed a corona of knotted herb plants, their fragrance scenting the air. There also, I surmised Doña Aurora's hand.

A large bouquet of artificial flowers blanketed Trinidad's casket. A dozen votive candles encircled his photograph, a stiffly formal portrait taken when the subject had been in his forties. In the picture he wore a black suit and smiled self-consciously.

I looked around the church and counted twenty-one members of Trinidad's family occupying the front five pews on the left. And those were only the ones who lived close enough to attend. A large and loving family, the Quirozes' attendance did not surprise me. It was the attendance for Rhea that raised my eyebrows. One by one the people moved forward to her casket, placed bunches of dried flowers or gifts of pottery and food at its base, murmured brief prayers, and kissed or stroked the casket in respect. One elderly woman, arms raised toward the heavens, slid down the aisle on her knees as if venerating a saint.

"The church is going to bust open if one more person tries to squeeze in," whispered Charlie as we crushed together to seat two new arrivals on our row.

"When Father Jack sees this crowd," Clay whispered in my ear, "he'll apply to the bishop to have Rhea beatified."

I nodded absently. I watched Robert Darke and Jessica Rex where they stood together by the door. Dignified in his dark suit, Robert appeared at his best. Jessica wore a suit of creamy gold. People had begun to speak of them as a couple.

Who was using whom in that relationship? Robert offered wealth and the prestige of social status. Was it enough for a woman like Jessica to play the trophy wife for a few years before she, too, was discarded?

I poked Clay in the ribs with my elbow.

He let out his breath in a whoosh, frowned questioningly at me, then followed my stare to the couple in the doorway. Any comment he might have made he stifled as the priest approached the altar.

As we rose to our feet, I glanced back one more time. Jessica saw me looking. No change in her expression. Would her expression change if she knew I had the photograph she had taken of Linden? Did it mean anything beyond a friendship that for whatever reason she had failed to acknowledge when her friend vanished? Would it worry her at all if I told her I would show it to the sheriff?

As the priest intoned, "The Lord be with you," I faced front and concentrated on the service. I had to give Father Jack credit. At least he'd taken the trouble to memorize the Mass in Spanish, unlike two of his predecessors.

I didn't spot Luke Fair until we followed behind the pallbearers in a procession to the cemetery. Luke stood off to one side, slightly behind the crowd of mourners. As his mother's casket was lowered, he eased forward and dropped in a wilted bouquet of flowers he'd been gripping, then slipped away as Father Jack recited a final prayer. From the edge of the crowd, I watched Luke move slowly toward the river, never looking back, his bony shoulders hunched with grief. He had lost his last connection to this side of the river.

After the interment, the crowd scattered quickly. The overeager visiting of far-flung relatives and neighbors that usually follows the obsequies had taken place the day before at fiesta. I paid my respects to the Quiroz family and left, meeting Billy at the cemetery gates and following him in my pickup on the hour-long drive to his parents' home.

At the time of her marriage, Maria's father, a wealthy man whose multinational company (the headquarters were in Mexico) held property on both sides of the river, deeded six thousand acres to her. "A bribe," Maria had said scornfully, "to keep my black husband away from the *hidalgo's* home."

The house, built before Maria had been born, was adobe, low and long, set in a basin of the upper mountains below Marfa. Rich land where cattle grazed on grama grass and thrived, and distant enough from El Polvo that, after Billy started high school in Presidio and Maria accepted the teaching post at our school, she had lived in the schoolhouse five days a week, going home only on weekends.

The first thing I saw when we entered the living room was a photograph that I had never seen before, an eight-by-ten color portrait of Maria and William posed together in front of the rambler rose by the front door. It brought tears to my eyes. How many times had I driven up here for a visit and been welcomed by the two of them, standing just as they were in the photograph.

Billy stood shifting his weight from one foot to the other and looking anywhere but at my face.

"Don't worry. I won't cry," I told him, sniffing and forcing back the tears. "Did Jessica Rex take that picture?"

He nodded. "She took that for me. The woman takes a lot better photos than most professionals. I guess anybody can take a picture. It's seeing what to take that's the hard part.'' He lightly touched the framed photo. "I'm glad I have this. Mom always liked the roses in bloom.''

I looked closer at the photograph. "Jessica took this last spring."

"Yes."

"She seems to be cropping up everywhere. Funny she never came into the trading post with the rest of the team."

"I think she stayed mostly at Mr. Darke's ranch and went places with him," Billy said, looking sheepish. "I asked her out once, you know. We went to dinner at La Escondida. She seemed to enjoy herself. We talked a lot. Well, mostly I did. She asked a lot of questions about my parents. Said she was interested in ranch life. So I invited her up for a visit. That's when she took that picture. Next time I called her for a date, she was very cool. I hear she's going to marry Mr. Darke.''

"Yes, that seems to be the consensus," I said. "I guess we'd better get on with our search, if it's still okay with you.''

I had told Billy in general what I wanted to search for: anything that Rhea Fair might have left with Maria for safekeeping, or a copy of a letter Maria might have written for her. He assumed my interest in the missing document had to do with settling Rhea's estate, an idea I didn't refute. Why worry Billy for no reason, if the search turned up nothing. And I admit I didn't want to acknowledge my real reason for the search. I was a little afraid that if I told him I was hoping to find a connection to the motive behind the murder of the *curandera,* he might laugh at me.

In spite of the fact that Maria had always told me she never intended to let *things* dominate her life, she had managed to accumulate the usual amount of possessions in terms of furniture, clothes, and dishes. Where Maria excelled in acquisitiveness was in her library. If she'd hidden what I hoped to find in a book, I'd be a long time looking, I thought as I surveyed the wide living room where books overflowed the shelves to smother the tabletops.

"We can start in Mom's office," Billy said, leading the way down the hall from which four bedrooms opened. At the end of the hall a twelve-by-twelve room was nearly filled by a large desk with an ancient upright typewriter on which Maria had pounded out countless letters-to-the-editor to newspapers across the state. Maria had believed in political activism and the power of the printed word and had practiced both. It would have been on this machine that she typed the letter for Rhea.

In Linden Fonda's apartment, I'd been an intruder prying into the privacy of another person. In Maria's office I felt at home. Here I had no worry that my search might be unwarranted, a journey into nosiness. Alive, Maria would have applauded my search for answers and would have helped me if she could.

In a little under two hours, Billy and I had scanned every carbon of every letter Maria had kept. Her files went back over ten years. Nowhere in her desk did we find a piece of paper pertaining to the *curandera*.

Having agreed to a search, Billy was thorough. We examined every drawer in the house where papers might be kept, including the chest of drawers and the desk in the kitchen, where we found only recipes.

Finally we searched his father's desk, which contained ranch records, tax receipts, bills—the normal paper trail that we leave in life. Nothing else.

Billy fixed us coffee and put together some cheese sandwiches and we ate lunch on the courtyard patio where Maria had grown cacti in pots and a precious collection of blooming annuals grown from seed that Maria had saved from one season to the next. The plants were browned and withered in their clay pots.

Billy looked gloomily at the dead flowers. "I should clean things up and pack away Mom and Dad's belongings, I guess."

"There's time enough. Maybe Annie can help you," I suggested, forgetting Clay's words of wisdom on that subject.

Billy shook his head. "No. Annie will leave here for good after her mother dies. She likes it out there," he added, shaking his head to rid himself of confusion the way a puppy might shake off water.

I understood that by "out there" he referred to the world beyond the border.

"It's funny, you know," he told me, his voice pensive. "I think if I ask her right now, she'd marry me. That would be a big mistake. I'm going to stay here, live in this house, and run the ranch. If we married and stayed here, she'd like me less and less each day until we'd end up strangers to each other. She despises all the things about this place I most love. The isolation. The quiet. The simplicity."

"Life in slow motion, my first husband called it."

Billy laughed. "I forgot. You know better than anyone what I'm talking about."

"I wasn't as smart as you. I didn't see that circumstance and place can be as important as whom you love. Not until it was almost too late.''

On that somber note, we finished our food and did the little washing-up required. I asked Billy if I could flip through some of the books on the chance that his mother might have left something in one. A little embarrassed at asking, I apologized for seeming obsessive.

Billy smiled warmly. "Mom always said you obsessed about all the right things."

Between us, we took down every book and shook it, hoping a paper would fly from between the pages. In four hours all we accomplished was to dust the shelves as we went.

I said good-bye to Billy and, discouraged, went out to my pickup. For no particular reason, I took the slower route back home on a ranch road that bumped and dipped its way down the mountain, coming out at El Polvo just behind the schoolhouse.

Though it was Saturday, a few children had congregated at the school, the younger ones sitting on the steps watching the older ones play kickball. Ned Little, the teacher, watched the play, a book held loosely in one hand. As I drove by, he raised a hand in silent greeting, and I waved back absentmindedly.

Half a mile farther down the road I did a U-turn.

Ned gave me a curious glance as I parked by his gold VW at the side of the whitewashed school.

The shouting voices of the children were a background noise, counting for little against the immense quiet in general. I walked over to Ned and asked if he had time to talk.

Ned is a genial young man who had served as a

teacher's aide for two years before assuming the teaching job full-time after Maria's murder. He lived in a tiny adobe in the back that had been long abandoned until Maria had asked for volunteers to fix it up for the school's use. With room and board to offer, but no salary, Maria had set about getting a volunteer to serve as a teacher's aide. Ned had been working in the Big Bend as a river raft guide. He heard about the opening, arrived in the middle of the day, and stayed, going back to his room at the park headquarters only to collect his gear. Romantic theories abound about why he stays on. That he is hiding from the law, running away from an unhappy love affair, setting up a smuggling operation, and so on. My theory is simple: He likes the place and the people.

I explained to Ned that I was trying to find some personal papers belonging to Maria and asked if he knew whether or not she might have left anything in the school files.

He smiled, jumped to catch the ball as it sailed toward the window of the school, and tossed it back to the little boy chasing it.

"There are some files in the bottom drawer, lesson plans and things she'd discarded. I went through most of it last summer. I seem to remember some odds and ends that weren't school-related. Come on. I'll show you."

Stepping inside the school always makes me feel I should head for the right rear desk, where I preferred to sit as a student. Some things never change. The thick adobe walls with the powdery coating of dust from the mud plaster. The smell of chalk. The stacks of books. The maps and charts on display.

I followed Ned into the workroom. The cot and hot plate Maria had used were gone. Still there were the scarred worktable, the copy machine she had bartered from the office supply house in Alpine, the reference books, school supplies, and neat stacks of textbooks.

Ned had pulled open the bottom drawer of one of two file cabinets. "Here we are," he said brightly. "If you don't find what you're looking for here, try any of the other files in this cabinet. These are the out-of-use files. If you need me, I'll be reading the kids a story."

I knelt down and picked through the stiff manila folders. The files weren't in alphabetical order, and they had been squeezed in tightly. But each was labeled in Maria's perfect printing. Halfway through I found it. A thin file labeled FAIR, R.

I took a deep breath, lifted it out, and quickly examined the contents. Then I sat cross-legged and read through them slowly. In the quiet of the school, with only the ticking of the wall clock for company, as I understood the import of the documents, my hands trembled. There were still questions to be answered, but what I had was a motive for Rhea's murder.

I reread the documents. Rhea's marriage license, a carbon of a letter typed on Maria's old typewriter, a newspaper clipping of a display advertisement. The last had come, I guessed, from one of the newspapers Rhea's patients had brought for her to use to start fires in her woodstove. There had been piles of them in her front room. She must have read some of them from time to time, and on one occasion, she had seen this ad.

"Find what you wanted?"

I jumped. Ned had come in behind me. I got up and grabbed his arm.

"I need to make copies of these papers," I said.

If he was surprised by my abruptness, he covered it well.

"You're in luck," he said. "The copier is working this week. It's old and somewhat undependable. How many copies do you want?"

I thought a minute. "Say, three of each."

"May I," he said, holding his hand out for the file. I gave it to him.

After a few adjustments to the copier, he finished the job quickly and sorted the papers into sets.

"What now?" he asked.

I didn't know. I thought it over. Keep the originals here, I decided. The killer hadn't realized Rhea had documented proof hidden safely in the school. That much was evident. I asked Ned to keep one set of the copies in his house. The other two I took with me.

As I left, I marveled that Ned had never once asked any questions, yet only a glance at the documents told the story. I wasn't worried. He was a quiet man who knew how to keep things to himself. He assumed I would do what needed to be done, and if anything happened to me, he would know what to do without my spelling it out for him now.

I hid my copies of the documents among the ledgers beneath the front counter of the trading post. Then I felt through the pockets of three jackets until

I found the bottle of herbal water and the packet of dried herbs that Doña Aurora had given me for protection against evil. The clairvoyant had said there would be one more death. Trinidad had since died, and perhaps that had been the death she meant, but I was taking no chances. I held the bottle in one hand, the packet in the other. Was it sprinkle the herbs and keep the herbal water with me or sprinkle the water and carry the herbs? I couldn't remember, so I tossed some of each in all four corners of the building and put the remainder on my dresser where it would be handy if I decided to carry it with me. It couldn't hurt, I assured myself. The odds were fifty-fifty it might help.

Afterward, I poured myself a generous whiskey, carried it to the porch, sat in one of the chairs, and put my feet up on the rail. The documents might be only circumstantial evidence, but I felt no doubt that I could name the person who had fired a gun into Rhea's face and burned her personal effects. Maria and her husband had been murdered in a similar manner—shot at close range—and their vehicle set on fire. Because the same person had killed them? I looked toward the cemetery. Only twelve days ago I had put flowers on their graves. I had work yet to do, information to look for before I felt certain enough of what I thought I knew to hand the information on.

But in my heart, I could name the killer. I sipped the whiskey and put my whole mind to planning my next step.

TWENTY

THREE TIMES over the next three days, I picked up the telephone to call Robert Darke, and three times I put the receiver down before anyone answered. Indecision was unusual for me, but any decision I made, anything I did, was going to cause pain.

Knowing I had only one realistic choice, I drove to the school and picked up the original set of documents I had left with Ned. After that, I called Andalon, then made the two-hour drive into Marfa to hand them, and the two photographs Jessica had taken of Linden Fonda, over to him.

Andalon told me to pull up a chair. He read through the documents with a grim, set face.

"This law firm that placed the ad—have you called them?" he asked.

"Of course not. They might have reacted too fast and upset your investigation. I want Rhea's murder solved first. You do think all this is related, don't you?" I said, pointing to the documents.

He agreed the items showed a motive for murder. "What we lack," he said, "is proof." He picked up Rhea's marriage license. "This Kingston Rex she married in high school—the name's familiar, but I can't place him."

"Are you going to call that law firm while I'm here or not?" I said.

He smiled. "Just wanted to hear you ask." He picked up the phone and dialed.

The part of the conversation I heard consisted of Andalon's request to speak to someone about the ad offering a reward for information about the whereabouts of Rhea Rex. After that Andalon said "Yes," "No," and explained he had a document that might be of interest to the law firm, but that he was investigating a murder and until he was given some information could say no more. For a long time he listened and took notes. He promised to be in touch with whomever he spoke to, then hung up and stared at me.

"What? What?" I said.

"Kingston Rex is now married to Gigi Rex, only child and heir of Cap Monahan, the founder of CapTex Oil and Exploration Company. Mrs. Rex has filed for divorce. Unfortunately for her, she had formed a partnership with her husband using a substantial part of her fortune. Since Texas is a community property state, after the divorce Kingston Rex would retain a half-share in the partnership. Ms. Monahan's lawyer reckons that would amount to roughly forty million dollars. I'd say that would be plenty of motive for murder."

I nodded. "Mattie Brant told me Jessica had a doting father and a rich stepmother."

"But," he said, "he'll lose every penny if the community property right is nullified by proof that Gigi Monahan and King Rex had never been legally married. Seems the lawyers think he failed to divorce his first wife, Rhea Hill Rex. According to the lawyer, Rex made and lost a couple of fortunes. The last in real estate. Right before he married the Monahan money, he filed for bankruptcy and just missed going to jail for fraud and embezzlement in connection with the failure of Crown Savings and Loan. Lawyer fees and court fines came to half a million dollars.''

I held up the carbon of the *curandera's* letter. ''With Rhea dead,'' I said, ''is this proof enough that they didn't divorce?''

''The lawyers will have to fight that out.''

''I don't understand why she had to be killed. She told Rex he was safe. She wasn't going to come forward.''

''How did she put it?'' Andalon said. ''The part about the court paper.''

I found the sentence and read it aloud. '''A piece of paper from some court wouldn't mean anything to me. We had no hard feelings when we agreed to go our separate ways and that's what matters.'''

''They were just kids when they married,'' Andalon said. ''Rex must not have seemed very real to her, after all these years. I wonder if she knew how much money he stood to gain?''

''She must have thought he had some money. Luke told me she thought about asking him for help when he and Matt were arrested,'' I said. ''I wonder how the present wife became suspicious that Rex hadn't bothered to divorce his first wife?''

''Poor chump probably told her himself. Or as soon as Gigi Monahan married him, her lawyers hired private detectives to dig into his past. I'll have to do a little digging about him myself. Now that you've handed me the motive, what I have to find is some concrete evidence linking Jessica Rex to

Rhea's murder. I need to make some calls to the police in San Antonio, then ask the judge for a warrant to search Jessica's vehicle and her rooms at the Darke ranch.''

I left him to his tasks and drove away feeling curiously deflated and depressed. I hadn't told Andalon of my belief that if Jessica had killed Rhea, she had also killed Maria and William. I hoped he'd come to that conclusion himself and find evidence to prove it. I went on to Alpine and talked to the editor of the *Avalanche,* who gave me the name of a reporter in Austin who could tell me what I needed to know and generously offered the use of the newspaper's telephone. The Austin reporter said there would be a file on Kingston Rex. I gave him Andalon's name and the address of the sheriff's office and asked him to send photocopies there. I had done all that I could. The rest was up to Andalon. I went home to wait.

TWENTY-ONE

ROBERT DARKE'S fiesta began at sundown, with the three hundred or so out-of-town guests mingling, chatting, and exchanging stories with the several hundred locals, and all drinking border buttermilk, a mix of tequila and lemonade. The mountain air chilled quickly after sunset, and guests moved between the house and the marquee tent set up for dancing. The buffet tables in the living area overflowed with tempting foods. The poker players gathered around tables in one of the guest rooms.

Clay and I stood on the lawn sipping our drinks and watching the parade of guests. The costuming was about half-and-half, black tie or Western. Suede, leather, embroidery, and denim dominated the western aficionados, with bolo ties for the men and turquoise by the pound for the women. Through the windows, we could see our host, with Jessica on his arm, as he moved among his guests in the brightly lit living room.

The wind picked up, swirling my long skirt around my legs and bringing the sound of Western swing our way. Against the white wall of the tent elongated shadows moved in a line dance. Clay put his arm around my shoulders and sipped at his drink with distaste.

The worthy Eliot Lofts, glass in hand and a smile on his face, marched across the lawn and joined us.

"The decibel levels of conversation are rising inside," he said, "to the point of affecting my hearing."

"Robert's annual fiestas are always great successes," I remarked.

"And I suppose this one will be even more of a celebration, considering Robert's personal happiness," Lofts said, glancing back toward the house.

The sound of laughter and snippets of conversation carried to where we stood. Clay's eyes met mine with a flicker of worry, and at that moment Mattie Brant exited the tent and walked over to join us.

The glass in her hand held clear liquid. Mineral water, I wondered, or straight tequila? Whichever, it wasn't helping her mood. She looked glum, with downcast eyes and drooping mouth.

Lofts greeted her warmly and said to us, "Mattie's leaving tomorrow, in spite of my efforts to persuade her to stay with the team for the windup work."

Mattie managed a smile. "Time for me to go home and decide what I'm going to do with my life," she said. Shivering in her light dress, she added, "It's cold out here."

"Let's go inside," Lofts said, and we trailed across the lawn and up the steps.

As we reached the door, Clay suggested fresh drinks.

Mattie wrinkled her nose and looked at our glasses.

"Not that foul stuff," she said.

Clay laughed. "I agree. Now that I've had the obligatory sip, let's find Robert's whiskey. I know for a fact he hates this stuff himself."

Lofts agreed with alacrity, and we made our way to the bar, lost the glasses we had, and requested whiskey. Except for Mattie, who held out her glass and asked for tequila.

Drinks in hand, we made our way to the far end of the room and sat down to talk.

Lofts prattled on happily about the findings of his team. Clay primed him with a series of questions that maintained the flow. Mattie's eyes shifted from the glass clutched in her hands to the figure of Robert Darke as he and Jessica worked one group of guests after another.

"I hear our host," a woman nearby remarked loudly to her companion, "is going to announce his engagement to that stunning young woman tonight."

Not now, I thought frantically. Not tonight.

Mattie's face looked pinched, her expression resentful.

"Is that true?" I asked Lofts.

He gave an uncomfortable glance at Mattie and said, "I did see cases of champagne being brought in this morning."

"You can take that as a yes," Mattie said. "Jessica's been triumphant all week." She sipped her drink, looked at us, then excused herself and hurried off. I watched her small figure weave through the crowd of guests.

"Strong feelings there," Lofts said. "She's a charming child, but she hasn't yet learned to dissemble. Wears her feelings on her sleeve, as they say. I hope things work out for the best."

"I hope so, too," I said, with something more than Mattie Brant's happiness in mind.

Robert Darke approached with Jessica and another couple. He made introductions and asked Lofts if he'd mind showing the couple the artifacts from the cave excavation. "They have a son who may want to join your team next season," Robert told him. Lofts departed with the pair to show and tell and sell.

The party swirled around us, louder and more relaxed by the minute. Robert said something to Jessica that I couldn't hear, and while she responded, Clay whispered in my ear, "He's a friend. We have to warn him."

I indicated agreement with a slight nod, reset my social face, and smiled.

Jessica Rex, in a satiny gown, looked beautiful. Her youth seemed a perfect foil to Robert's maturity. In her manner, also, was more confidence. The diffidence I had assumed went with a shy personality had vanished, replaced with an unexpected social ease. And something more. Mattie's comment about her triumphant attitude had not been grounded in only her own envy. In voice, gesture, and expression, Jessica declared herself in possession of Robert and his home.

While I pondered the change in Jessica's personality, Clay tried to get Robert aside. First he suggested a quick word with Robert about the possibility of a rabies vaccine airdrop, but Robert didn't bite, telling Clay he'd give him all the time in the world for business the next day.

Clay ad-libbed gamely, asking Jessica to dance. She excused herself by saying that Robert and she still had newly arriving guests to welcome. "Perhaps later,'' she told him. They spun away from us and continued circulating among their guests.

He took a long drink and turned to me. ''What now?''

''The party's just getting started. Maybe one of us will get a chance to talk to him later.''

''I think I'll visit the buffet and cushion the whiskey with some food,'' Clay said.

''You always eat in times of travail,'' I said.

''Join me?''

I shook my head. ''You go ahead. I think I'll try and find Mattie and see if she can help us corner Robert.''

I wandered around, feeling unsociable, regretting my failure to speak with Robert earlier in the week.

Twenty minutes later, Robert made me a gift of the opportunity to talk with him privately.

''Come with me, Texana,'' he said, touching my elbow. ''I want to show you something.'' He guided me to the library.

With its leather armchairs and Turkish rugs, the room made the perfect backdrop for Robert's easy masculinity.

Before I could say a word, Robert went to his desk, picked up a mounted photograph, and handed it to me, smiling broadly.

It was a print of the picture of me that Jessica had taken in the cave.

''Well?'' he said. ''Don't you like it?''

''It's the best picture I've ever had taken,'' I said truthfully. ''I like it very much.''

I looked at Robert's familiar face, so genial and happy in the moment. I was about to end all that.

Would he listen to what I had to say and believe me, or was I about to lose a friend? A man whom I genuinely liked. A man who had done so much for Clay. For the community. I put the photo down on the desk.

"I need to have a talk with you, Robert," I told him.

Puzzled but polite, Robert stood waiting for me to speak.

I didn't know how to begin.

"Robert..." I said. "I'm sorry... I don't... I'm afraid what I have to say will hurt you."

He frowned and a hint of impatience fought with puzzlement on his face. His innate good manners overwhelmed both.

"Tell whatever is bothering you, Texana, and let me sort it out."

He made it sound so simple. I had nothing with me to show him, not even the duplicate documents. Nothing but my own words. Would that be enough?

"Are you going to speak?" he said.

I did. I marshaled my thoughts into some sort of coherence and told him what I suspected. That Jessica might have knowledge about Rhea's murder and the disappearance of Linden Fonda. That alive, the *curandera* was a threat to Jessica's father. That the *curandera's* death meant great gain for Jessica through her father, and Jessica had been aware of this.

His first reaction was dismissive anger. What was I thinking, he asked me in a fierce tone, making such accusations? Talking such nonsense?

To help you, I thought. To spare you public embarrassment, if not private unhappiness. Suddenly I wished to be anywhere but there. I should have waited for Andalon to do his job. Should have left Robert to his fate. Now it was too late. I had to face the consequences of my actions just as Robert did of his. Too late for compassion. For either of us.

I reiterated what I had told him. As the extent of what I implied sank in, his expression changed from disbelief to anguish. His eyes never left my face, never flinched. He didn't lack the courage to face the truth, only the will, as yet, to accept it.

I told him exactly what I knew and how I had learned it. Explained in detail the documents I had found.

He listened in silence, then moved slowly to a chair and sat down.

I had always thought Robert's feelings to be as insubstantial and skin-deep as the beauty of his various wives. Now I wondered if I had misjudged the man. His pain seemed real enough, his sense of betrayal acute.

"You say you can show me these documents? Why didn't you bring them with you?" he said.

"I didn't know you were going to announce your engagement at the fiesta. Otherwise, I'd hardly pick a social event to tell you such a thing." I heard the misery in my voice. Did he?

"But you say in this letter that Mrs. Fair wrote to Jessica's father, she assured him he had nothing to worry about," he said.

"Yes."

"Then Jessica had no reason—"

"Perhaps Jessica didn't believe her. Perhaps her father didn't."

In his face doubt fought with credulity.

I tried again. "As long as the *curandera* was alive, she might change her mind. Or someone might make the connection between Rhea Fair and the first Mrs. Rex. The *curandera* had a growing reputation for healing. People came from El Paso to see her. Linden Fonda planned a book about her. How long until someone found out? How long until someone claimed the reward for the information?"

He rose, moved to a window, and stood staring out. His thoughts took time. I could hear the wall clock ticking away the minutes. What was going through his mind? Finally, he turned back to face me.

"Have you shown the documents to anyone else?"

"I gave everything to the sheriff."

Robert lifted his head. "He's not here tonight. He was invited but he didn't come."

"No, Andalon wouldn't want to enjoy your hospitality tonight and then show up with a search warrant tomorrow or the next day."

Oddly, this bit of information seemed to finally convince him of the truth of what I had been saying. He looked down and slowly nodded his head.

The library door opened and Jessica came in.

"Here you are," she said. "Our guests are missing their host—" She stopped, halted by the look on Robert's face.

"It can't be true," Robert said. His voice shook. The words meant nothing. His tone lacked all conviction.

Jessica turned to me with a questioning glance.

"Leave us, please, Texana," Robert said. It was an order.

"You won't..." I said helplessly. Wishing Andalon was there. Wondering if I had ruined his investigation. Daunted by the thought that I had forced Robert to choose between two wrongs: Betray Jessica or betray justice.

I left them alone together.

TWENTY-TWO

THE LIBRARY DOOR shut noiselessly behind me. I stood in the hall trembling. My anxiety over what might happen next tempered my relief at being out of that room. I breathed deeply to calm myself.

My body stopped shaking. That left only my mind in a panic. What to do next? Find Clay? Stay near the library to see what happened when Robert and Jessica came out? Telephone Andalon and tell him what I'd done? If he had a timetable for his investigation, I'd accelerated it into high speed.

I returned to the living room. The convivial crowd had grown as the dancers had abandoned the tent for the buffet. I worked my way around the room, looking for Clay. My progress was slowed by friends wanting to chat. I made an effort to smile agreeably, but I kept moving. In the middle of the room, I ran into Charlie sipping a soft drink.

"Clay's looking all over for you," he said.

"I'm looking for him," I said.

"He was over by the corner, there, when I saw him," Charlie said.

I thanked him and headed in the direction he'd last seen Clay. Still, it took me some minutes to find him.

"I've been trying to find Robert," he said, looking harried.

"I know where he is. It's too crowded to talk here," I said. We made a creeping progression to the edge of the room and out to the front entrance. We walked a few paces from the house. The moon was full and up, its light nearly bright enough to read by.

"I've talked to Robert," I said.

Before Clay could ask one question, I told him what had happened. "Jessica's with him now," I said. "I'm afraid he's going to tell her." We stared miserably at each other.

"We have to let Andalon know," Clay said.

"You call him. I'll go keep an eye on the library door from the end of the hall."

"As long as you don't do anything but watch."

"I think I've done too much already. Robert has a vested interest in handling this without fanfare. Jessica's best option is denial. Nothing's going to happen. Go call."

He left, and I started back to stand watch. Halfway there, a wave of nausea hit me. Cursing border buttermilk, I turned and made for the far end of the guest wing and a bathroom. Lucky for me, it was empty. I splashed cold water on my face and neck and felt better. I stepped out into the hall and came face-to-face with Jessica coming out of the room opposite. She had changed into slacks and a turtleneck sweater and clutched a duffel bag in her hand. I have never seen a look of such pure hatred as the one she gave me. It dissolved her beauty into an ugly mask. I experienced the same feeling of hollow fear I got every time I saw a rattlesnake.

I glanced down the hallway. Empty. At almost the same moment, she stepped toward me, reached into the bag, brought out a gun, and pointed it at my stomach.

"You've destroyed everything I've worked for and you're going to pay for it."

She positioned the duffel bag so it hid the automatic from view of anyone coming from the main room into the guest wing. Her eyes, staring straight into mine, were gleaming ice.

"Everything I did, all that time, and planning, and effort," she hissed. "For nothing. You…you interfering *bitch*."

I knew I should do something. Run. Shout. I felt frozen. Body and mind disengaged. When I spoke, I didn't recognize my own voice.

"Think of all those people out there. If you shoot me, they'll hear. You can't get away."

Her eyes flickered with malice and arrogance.

She's going to kill me right here, I thought.

"We're going outside. Walk ahead of me," she said, coming closer and motioning toward the near end of the hall. I walked, and we went out a door that led past the stables toward the five-car garage. The open parking bays were lit and each held one of Robert's Suburbans. I knew for a fact that Robert left the keys in for convenience, and because, here, it was safe to do so.

"This one," Jessica said as we approached the first bay. "You drive."

I hesitated and felt the gun shoved against my spine.

"Jessica!"

We both turned. Mattie Brant, her eyes soft-focused from too much tequila, stood at the end of the car staring at us. And then her eyes dropped to the gun in Jessica's hand.

"Run, Mattie!" I shouted, shoving Jessica with all my strength. The gun went off.

I saw Mattie stagger backward. I heard a man's voice, from somewhere outside, shout, "What the hell!" Jessica bolted past me and was gone.

I didn't realize I'd been shot until I felt the warm blood soaking into the side of my dress. Knowledge brought burning pain, and I sank to the ground.

Then, Mattie was standing over me yelling for help. The bay filled with people, one of whom pushed past Mattie and knelt beside me. "I'm a doctor," he said.

"Need any help with the patient, David?" said someone else.

I felt immensely grateful that Robert's guest list always included a number of doctors. That reminded me.

"Someone go to the library," I said. "Robert may be hurt."

The man called David gave me a sharp look. I heard someone else say, "I'll go." David probed my side with his hand. I felt a sharp pain, my vision went gray and fuzzy, and I fainted.

TWENTY-THREE

SITTING AMID cushions on a chaise longue in one of the Darke guest rooms and floating in a euphoric state induced by a pain pill, I barely felt either my broken rib or the deep bruising where the bullet had grazed my side. The drapes had been pulled against the late afternoon sun and the room was dim. Clay sat in a chair by the bed and held my hand. Robert wandered around the room. Andalon and Charlie sat in chairs at a table on which a folder of documents lay open.

"So Jessica did get into Linden Fonda's apartment?" Robert said.

"Your pilot flew her into San Antonio on the sixth of November," Andalon said. "He waited at the airport. She rented a car and was gone for four hours. Plenty of time to search Fonda's apartment and ditch the things she took from there."

"I remember," Robert said. "She told me she had to go home to get some clothes and pick up some film."

"She covered herself," Andalon said. "The pilot said she came back with a garment bag and a case of film. The San Antonio cops are checking the pawnshops for Fonda's computer."

"If they find a computer, how will they know it's the right one?" Charlie asked.

Andalon smiled. "They won't. They'll ask if a

terrific-looking blonde woman hocked it. My guess is she probably threw the computer, and anything else she took, into the nearest Dumpster.''

Charlie picked up a page from the folder. "Forty million dollars," he said, staring at the paper. "No wonder the woman committed murder.''

Robert looked stricken.

"I checked her Suburban this morning," Andalon said. "The license plate is registered to Rex, but the motor registration number matches the rental agency's missing vehicle.''

"So she switched plates," Clay said. "She'd been driving the Suburban Fonda rented.''

Andalon nodded. "She pried off the rental agency's metal logo and used a bumper sticker to cover the holes where the plate had been attached. My guess is that Rex used Fonda to get close to Mrs. Fair, then shot her either before or after she shot the *curandera*.''

"Where's Linden Fonda's body?" I asked.

"Dumped in a ravine anywhere between the line shack and here," Andalon said.

"We know Jessica drove Fonda's car back here after the murders and kept using it like it was another of the ranch's Suburbans," Charlie said, "but how'd she get to Mrs. Fair's place? It's miles across rough country. She couldn't have walked it, and if she had driven, that would mean she had to make two trips, one in Fonda's Suburban, one in the vehicle she'd driven herself.''

"Remember the horse Robert reported missing?" Andalon said. "The one that came back on its own with an injured leg?''

"Of course," Clay said. "She rode."

"And hid the horse in the brush while she approached the line shack," Andalon said. "That way, there was no vehicle to park on the ranch road below the line shack, where if someone passed it was sure to be noticed and remembered. That's the kind of thing, out here, no one's going to overlook or forget about."

"What happened, I wonder," Clay said, "that she drove the Suburban back and left the horse?"

"Either the horse bolted or she left it untied," Andalon said. "She had to get back to the ranch, so she had to take the Suburban. When she got back here, she switched the plates of her own vehicle—the one she drove out here from San Antonio—and the Suburban. She figured rightly that if we were looking for a Suburban with rental plates, we wouldn't check the plates on other model vehicles. Since she'd been driving one of the ranch Suburbans back and forth to the cave site every day, no one noticed anything. You have to admire a cool head."

"Mr. Darke," Charlie said, "you didn't notice the extra Suburban?"

Robert said, "At any one time, Eliot Lofts or the team members had almost all of the Suburbans out except the one I use personally. Other than making sure the ranch hands keep the vehicles clean and washed and ready for guests, I rarely concern myself with them. And none of the hands was likely to question what a guest of mine was driving."

"Rex lucked out with the missing Suburban. It confused the issue of why Mrs. Fair was murdered," Andalon said. "I suspected that either Fonda had killed Mrs. Fair for some personal reason and fled to Mexico herself, or that drug smugglers had killed both women and taken the Suburban. Fonda's missing body could be accounted for in a number of ways: She was shot, but managed to get away, only to die in the brush somewhere. The smugglers forced her to go with them for some distance and assaulted her before killing her and dumping the body."

"Jessica blamed the whole thing on this Linden Fonda," Robert said. "Last night, after I told her what Texana had told me, she admitted knowing Fonda. And she admitted knowing that Rhea Fair was legally her father's wife. But she claimed to know nothing about the *curandera's* murder. She said when Fonda turned up missing, she kept quiet about having known her to protect her father and keep him from losing everything. She said she was afraid to involve herself in anything to do with Rhea Fair because of her father's situation." He paused, came over to the bed, and looked down at me. "I'm sorry, Texana. If I hadn't weakened and believed her lies, you wouldn't have been hurt. She told me she was going to her room to change clothes so we could go and see Andalon together and get things cleared up immediately."

"You were being loyal to someone you loved, Robert. You have nothing to be sorry for."

"I've found out some things about Jessica's father, Kingston Rex, the past few days," Andalon said, "thanks to Texana's arranging for me to get some clippings from the *Austin American-Statesman*. The paper did a profile on 'King' Rex, as they called him, when Cap Monahan's daughter filed for divorce. As a young man he worked in the oil fields as a pumper. He put his savings and a small inheritance from his mother into a risky gas well that came in big. Much later he lost a lot of money in the Austin chalk exploration. In his thirties, he married twice. Jessica is his daughter by his second wife, that is if we don't count Mrs. Fair. Right now he's a sick old man, weakened by a stroke brought on, the newspaper implied, by the stress of contesting the divorce.''

Robert went to the table and looked down at the picture of Rhea that had run with the ad seeking information about her whereabouts. "I would never have recognized her," he said, "from that picture."

Andalon said, "No one out here knew Mrs. Fair until she was in her thirties. This had to be a high-school picture. What would lawyers and law officers do without yearbooks? And who would think to connect an old woman living in a line shack with the scandal of a Houston oil family?"

I closed my eyes and let my head drop back against the pillows, drained of all energy. My emotions fluctuated between relief at being alive and disgust that Jessica Rex had escaped.

"Right now, Jessica is safe in Mexico," I said.

"My fault," Robert said.

I sat up. "No. Mine. If I hadn't told you—"

"You two argue over taking the blame some other time," Andalon said. "Charlie here gets the credit for seeing Jessica getting on a horse and for finding Robert's pilot so they could take off and circle until they spotted her making for the border."

"Charlie and Mattie were the night's heroes," I

said. "I wish Mattie hadn't left so early. I didn't have a chance to thank her for saving my life."

"She seemed to think you saved her life," Andalon said.

"Why did she follow Jessica and me to the garage?"

"She didn't," Clay said. "She'd had too much to drink. She went outside to clear her head, saw you and Jessica, decided it was time to tell Jessica what she thought of her—that was the liquor working— and came after you. Thank God."

"Why didn't Jessica take one of the other hundred or so vehicles belonging to the guests?" I said.

"After that shot brought half the party running," Andalon said, "Jessica made for the closest place— the stables. I guess she figured Mexico was close, too, and that her best chance was in that direction. Once on the other side, I couldn't touch her. Plus after she shot you, she could hardly drive out. She must have known that I'd be notified of what had happened and be waiting on the road to stop her, with the border patrol waiting in the opposite direction. And if she got past me, there was still the highway patrol to get past. It isn't like she had a lot of choices of escape routes out here."

"She made it to Mexico," I said. "She's safe."

"She's in Mexico," Andalon said. "But safe? Only if she has money and friends there. If not, God help her."

TWENTY-FOUR

TWO DAYS LATER I felt well enough to walk to Doña Aurora's house. A young couple carrying a baby were leaving as I arrived. The front room smelled of oil and herbs. The clairvoyant had been giving a blessing.

Sitting on the edge of her bed, her white hair fluffed around her wrinkled face, Doña Aurora greeted me with affection. I sat beside her, and she patted my hand and peered at me over her glasses.

"You didn't do as I told you and keep the herbs with you."

"How did you know?"

"If you had done as I said, you wouldn't have been hurt. Now, you need my help again, but I cannot tell you what you want to know."

"You know what I'm going to ask?"

"I sense it. You want to know whether I can help you find the lost woman. You fear she is dead, but you are not sure."

Doña Aurora grasped my hand, her grip firm.

She closed her eyes and breathed evenly and deeply for some moments. Then her eyes flew open and she shook her head.

"Nothing," she said. "I see nothing."

"Does that mean she's dead?"

She fingered the blue plastic cross at the end of

her rosary. "I don't know. Maybe it means only that she's not lost. I can't see more. I'm sorry."

It was hopeless, I thought. I would never know what happened to Linden Fonda.

Doña Aurora's voice was blessing me and then I was out the door and walking back to the trading post. With each step her words drummed in my mind... "Not lost...not lost."

I stepped up my pace. When I reached the trading post I went straight to the wall map of the county and traced my finger along the track from Rhea Fair's line shack to the Darke Ranch. Halfway between, the track passed the tail end of the canyon where Jesse Waites had his silver trailer.

I banged out the back door and marched to Clay's trailer, opened the screen door, and looked past the waiting room and into his office at the right. He sat with his feet propped on the desk.

"Are you busy?" I asked.

He raised his eyes from the veterinary science manual on his lap.

"Not if you need me," he said. He looked so content, I almost felt guilty. But not enough.

"Did you ever check on Jesse Waites? He didn't show up at our fiesta."

Clay swung his feet to the floor and put the book on his desk. "I'd forgotten about Jesse," he said, a frown creasing his forehead. "I need to get up there and make sure he hasn't been bitten by a coyote. Thanks for reminding me."

"I want to go with you."

He turned from reaching for his vet's kit to look

at me. "You sure you feel like it? It's a rough drive to get near his trailer."

"I'll meet you at the pickup," I said. "You have the gun, don't you? In case he's taken in some stray dog that's rabid?"

"I always carry the pistol in the pickup," he said. "You know that."

I nodded and went to change shoes for the trip. I also filled a jug of water and packed a box of canned goods and a bottle of whiskey for the old man. Might as well save him a trip in to the trading post, I thought.

We left the blacktop, climbed the track until it ended, and bumped and bounced over the desert as it rose to meet the mountains. My side felt every jolt, and I regretted not taking a pain pill before leaving home.

"What do you expect to find at Jesse's?" Clay asked me, his eyes intent on the terrain ahead.

"Remember you told me that Jesse might have bought the penicillin for himself and not livestock?"

Clay nodded.

"Well, I think maybe he bought it to use on someone else."

I watched his face as he thought it over.

"My God!" he said, turning his head long enough to give me a quick stare. "You expect to find Linden Fonda at Jesse's."

"Not expect, exactly. But I'd like to see for myself. Wouldn't you?"

"You bet."

We drove a little farther, and he said, "Open that glove compartment and get out the gun."

The terrain roughened and our option of continuing by four-wheel drive ran out. Foot power would get us the rest of the way. Clay lifted out his vet kit, put the pistol in his holster, and picked up the box of supplies, carrying it under one arm. I carried the whiskey.

Clay climbed the narrow footpath ahead of me; the one with the gun always goes first to kill the snakes.

As we neared the silver trailer, Clay, some feet ahead of me, came to a stop.

"Look," he said in a somber voice.

I raised my eyes from watching where I stepped. Jesse's trailer is at the narrow end of the canyon's basin, nestled in a cup formed by rock-face walls on three sides. In the tops of the trees that grew in the rich, captured soil of the basin, five vultures perched, shrugging their shoulders and stretching their wings to meet the sun.

"Probably, they're just roosting," I said with more calm than I felt. In my gut, I was terrified we were going to find another body.

Clay brought out his pistol. He took three steps forward and a shot rang out, the bullet singing high over our heads. We both hit the dirt at the same moment that Jesse's raspy voice called out, "Goddammit, stay the hell out!"

"Well, at least we know he's not dead," Clay said, hugging the ground.

I tried to hand Clay the bottle of whiskey. "Wave this at him."

"Like hell."

"Jesse," I shouted, "it's Texana Jones. From the trading post."

"Who?" came a responding shout.

"Old buzzard couldn't buy a hearing aid," Clay mumbled. He made a megaphone of his hands and called up to Jesse, so loudly the words echoed back.

"It's Clay Jones. The vet."

"Who's the other fellow?" Jesse shouted back.

"My wife."

"Come on up," the old man called back.

Jesse met us at the edge of the half-acre clearing around his trailer. He'd put the rifle down across the arms of the sunburned red recliner where he did his drinking. A box of empties sat beside the dilapidated chair.

I handed him the new bottle of whiskey.

His face lighted up. "Say, thanks," he said. "Sorry about shooting at you, but I like my privacy and I don't like strangers."

Clay started to explain about the rabies outbreak and how he wanted to be sure Jesse hadn't picked up any stray livestock.

I interrupted. "Is she still here, Jesse?" I asked.

In the moment of silence that followed I could hear the dry sound of the wind moving up the canyon, making little eddies in the grass as it passed.

A strained voice came from the shadowed doorway of the trailer: "I know you, don't I? You're the woman from the trading post."

TWENTY-FIVE

FACED WITH the thing he most avoided—company—Jesse insisted in playing host by serving us lunch. He unloaded the box of supplies and made peanut butter sandwiches, washed down with whiskey for Clay and Jesse. Linden Fonda and I stuck to water.

We ate outside, since Jesse's trailer had room for one person to turn around—if he keeps his elbows down. Jesse helped Linden to his red recliner, then unearthed a plastic milk crate for me and a wooden box for Clay. Three chairs for company, Jesse said. All anyone needed. He sat cross-legged on the ground.

I wouldn't have recognized Linden Fonda, not from our brief meeting when she bought gas, nor from the fine photograph Jessica had taken. She wore the same shirt she had on when she stopped for gas, with a pair of pants that were obviously Jesse's. She had dark circles beneath her eyes, her shoulders were stooped, and she had lost weight. By her own admission, the harsh physical changes in the young woman had not occurred as the aftereffects of the gunshot wound in her arm.

"Bullet went right through," Jesse explained. "I cleaned it, stitched it closed with thread, and pumped her full of penicillin. Took me back to my tour of duty as an army medic."

"I've been so afraid Jessica would find me," she

said as Clay, the nearest thing to a doctor, examined the shiny hard surface of the scar left by the bullet. Linden rolled down her sleeve. "I haven't been able to eat or sleep since Jesse found out Mrs. Fair was dead. I feel so responsible."

Anxiety and guilt had made Linden ill.

"I didn't know what to do," she kept saying. She seemed to assume that we knew all about what had happened to her.

"She's a good kid," Jesse said. "She just don't feel able to cope. Feels like the world shifted and she's out of place. That's how I felt after I got home from Korea. I told her she could have the trailer till she got her head straight. Me, I'm used to sleeping under the stars. I throw down a blanket right here and sleep like a baby every night."

I leaned forward to look Linden in the eye, saying gently, "Jessica has run away to Mexico. We know she murdered Mrs. Fair. Is she the one who shot you?"

She nodded and her eyes filled with tears. "She came out of the brush."

"Hadn't we better start at the beginning?" Clay said.

"When I got to Mrs. Fair's?" Linden said.

"Why you came out here to see her," I suggested.

"Mrs. Fair wrote to me," Linden said. "Her schoolteacher friend had died, she said, and she wanted me to advise her. She was afraid of Jessica. She called her a witch and said something about Jessica putting the evil eye on her."

"Did you tell Jessica about the letter?" I said.

She nodded. "I thought...she was my friend."

"And if her father lost his divorce settlement because of Mrs. Fair, Jessica would suffer, too," I said.

"You know about that?"

"Yes."

Linden hugged herself and rocked slightly in the chair. "I was...I thought she should know. Mrs. Fair said in her letter she wanted to ask me some questions about Jessica. I felt sorry for Jessica. When her father lost his money the first time, it was so hard for her. She said she never wanted to be poor again. I understood. I was raised in poverty."

"Did Jessica know you planned to write a book about Mrs. Fair?" Clay asked.

"I told her. It was going to be an expansion of my thesis. The university press was going to publish it."

"So you answered Mrs. Fair's letter and arranged the visit," I said.

"Yes. Jessica told me to find out what Mrs. Fair wanted. She called her 'that filthy old woman.' Jessica said no one would live like Mrs. Fair if they didn't have to. She thought Mrs. Fair would keep quiet until her father's divorce settlement, then blackmail him. I didn't think so, but I promised Jessica I'd do what I could to find out."

I reached out and put my hand on Linden's. "Tell us what happened at the line shack." I could feel the quaking of her body beneath my fingers. When she spoke, her voice was so low I could hardly hear her.

"Mrs. Fair was expecting me. She was glad to see me. I gave her the groceries. Before we could talk, a Mexican man came to the door begging for water. Mrs. Fair told him he could get water at the spring, but he didn't have a container, so she gave him one.

Then she said as long as she had to show him the way, she'd collect water for herself. She got some milk jugs to hold the water. They went up the path."

"Why didn't you go with them?" Clay asked.

Linden shrugged. "They didn't need me, and Mrs. Fair told me to relax after the long drive," Linden said. "It was too stuffy inside. I waited outside."

Her voice had tightened on the last words. "Is that when Jessica came out of the brush, as you said?" I asked.

"Yes. She had a gun, and I asked her why. She said it was for snakes and laughed. She told me to go in the house. Then she went up the path." Linden squeezed her eyes shut.

"And then?" I said.

"When I heard the first shot, I ran back outside. There was another shot, and the Mexican came running down the path, shouting something in Spanish. He ran across the clearing and into the brush. It happened so fast. I was staring after him when I heard Jessica say my name."

She gave a shudder. Jesse got up and awkwardly patted her shoulder. Clay, more practical, poured a shot of whiskey and handed it to her. She gulped it down without choking and continued her story.

"She shot me. I couldn't believe it. I looked at my arm and saw the blood. She stepped closer and took aim again. And then the Mexican burst out of the brush and charged her. Jessica spun around to face him. I ran. I heard another shot. I kept going."

"The man who saved you tried to, too," I told her. "He tried to get back to the other side. He made it as far as the river before he collapsed and died."

Linden made a mewing sound. "I didn't know," she said, "which direction to go, the cactus was so thick. I crawled into the grass under a mesquite thicket. For a long time I heard Jessica calling my name. Then this awful-looking white dog tried to get at me. It came out of nowhere, snarling and drooling. It tried to claw its way through the thicket, but it couldn't get to me. Then it ran away. I think it saved me from Jessica though, because I heard it barking and growling, and then I heard Jessica cursing. I guess the dog scared her off and kept her from coming in my direction. I was afraid of the dog. I was glad it never came back to where I was."

"You were right to be scared," Clay told her. "The dog had rabies and bit one person that we know of. If it had gotten to you, it would have bitten you, too."

She nodded mutely, looking down at the knotted hands in her lap as if they belonged to someone else.

"After the dog went away, I kept still. It seemed like forever. Finally, I heard a car start, and I wondered if Jessica was taking my Suburban. The sound seemed to move up beyond the house, but I was so turned around, I couldn't be sure of the direction. I crawled out of the thicket and started walking in the direction that I thought would take me away from the house. I was afraid to go up the track or down to the road because I thought Jessica might be waiting there for me."

"That crazy woman's been up this canyon a couple of times since on horseback, nosing around," Jesse said. "That's how come I started playing the drunk old man sitting in the recliner and taking potshots at folks.''

"But how did you get here?" Clay asked Linden.

Jesse answered for her. "I found her late that day. I was out hunting, and there she was. Just wandering."

Clay smiled at Jesse. "Thinning out the game on the Darke Ranch?"

Jesse grinned. "I wasn't far over the fence. Mr. Darke will stock his place with exotics. I figure every one of those I kill makes room for one more mule deer. I'm a conservationist of native species."

"Did Mrs. Fair know that Jessica was her first husband's daughter?" I asked Linden.

"As far as I know, Mrs. Fair knew Jessica only as a photographer for some pet project of a local rancher named Robert Darke. Jessica met him at a charity party and found out he was from this area. She asked him to let her visit his ranch. She told him she wanted to photograph ranch life—cowboys, roundups, that sort of thing. She told me he was a pushover for young blondes. I guess she was right. In no time, he'd hired her to take pictures for this project of his. She said he had money, but not as much as she'd inherit if her father could hang on to his share of his wife's money. In spite of what she said, I assumed Jessica liked Robert Darke, but I've been thinking about it since. I guess she used him to have a reason to stay and keep an eye on Mrs. Fair.''

"When did Jessica find out that Mrs. Fair was her father's legal wife?" I asked.

"Last spring. She knew last spring. I don't know how."

"Mrs. Fair saw the ad," I said, "and wrote to Kingston Rex to tell him he had nothing to fear from her. I've seen a copy of the letter. Rhea says in the letter that Maria Deed helped her write the letter and typed it for her. Three weeks after the date on the letter, someone shot and killed Maria and her husband."

"I didn't know that," Linden said hoarsely. The horror in her face seemed genuine. She started to cry. Jesse looked uncomfortable.

I went on. "Rhea's personality played into Jessica's hands. She was too shy to talk about her personal business with most of the people she knew. That and her poverty kept her isolated. I think Jessica so desperately wanted to find out what Rhea might do that she tried to befriend her, taking her picture, going to visit her with Robert. It didn't work. Rhea kept her at arm's length. When Rhea wrote to you asking questions, Jessica acted. After she'd killed Rhea and tried to kill you, she searched Rhea's house, found an old picture of her father and Rhea together, and burned it along with Rhea's few other mementos. She was safe. Except for you. Your getting away was her only mistake. She stayed here all this time because of you. Riding out to search. Hoping you died of exposure, hoping to find your remains so she could be sure."

Clay touched my shoulder. "It's getting late and we have to notify Andalon."

Linden Fonda appeared so ill that we agreed she should stay where she was until Andalon could make arrangements to have her picked up by helicopter.

Clay and I left Jesse helping the weeping woman back inside the trailer.

"She'll need a hospital stay," Clay said as we walked down the canyon path.

On the drive home, I leaned back against the seat and closed my eyes, my stamina evaporated.

"I thought I'd feel better if I could find Linden," I said. "You know, all that crap about closure."

"But you don't?"

"I feel as if Rhea and Maria and William died yesterday," I said, putting my head on Clay's shoulder and wiping away tears. "And that poor man who saved Linden's life. He may never be identified or his body claimed. His family in Mexico may never know what happened to him. Maybe I should never have stirred all this up. Rhea was right. Let the past go."

"You're suffering battle fatigue," Clay said, putting his arm around my shoulders. "What would Maria have said?"

I thought a minute. "She once told me that the easiest way to betray the past is by failing to face the problems of the present. She was talking about her Spanish-Indian heritage and political activism, but somehow I think her statement fits my situation, too. If I hadn't wanted to resolve the deaths of my friends, it would have been a denial of their lives."

TWENTY-SIX

IN A DETAILED and rambling statement to Andalon and the district attorney, Linden Fonda nicely skewered her old friend, and a warrant was issued for the arrest of Jessica Rex for the murder of Rhea Fair.

A lie detector test had been ambiguous about whether or not Linden Fonda really had nothing to do with the murder of Rhea Fair or those of Maria and Bill Deed. "Her feelings of guilt," the psychiatrist hired by her lawyer said, "made the results inconclusive."

"As inconclusive as the diagnosis of a psychiatrist can be," Clay commented when Andalon told us the news.

But no matter how strong the evidence against Jessica Rex, it was useless unless she could be found. Andalon sent word to the sheriff of Chihuahua state in Mexico, and the Presidio County district attorney requested that federal authorities pressure Mexico for her capture and return. But, as Andalon pointed out, history was on her side.

"Crossing the border," he said, "has protected criminals from both sides for generations. Maybe someday the politicians will work it out. Until then, we local folks just have to sit on our hands."

Billy Deed didn't think much of that option. He resigned as constable and put up a five-thousand-dollar reward for information on the whereabouts of the murderer of his parents. Joe Quiroz helped pass the word on the other side.

I took the only action I could think of. I told the Letter Man to tell Luke Fair's friend Efrain about Jessica Rex. It was my way of passing the information to Luke.

Nothing happened.

As the weeks passed, the almost unbearable fact that the killer would not be returned for arrest and trial grew to all-absorbing proportions in our minds.

Only Clay, busy with greater worries, had little time to ponder the whereabouts of Jessica Rex. The governor had named him to a special commission to recommend ways of checking the spread of canine rabies in coyotes. This required that he spend three days of every month in Austin for meetings. During the rest of each month, he prepared written reports and practiced his arguments on me.

He had time for such things because the peak of the rabies outbreak in our area had passed. Each day he received fewer and fewer calls about exposed or sick animals. Tragically the number of human victims still climbed. The latest was an eleven-year-old girl who had died of the disease without her parents ever knowing how she contracted it.

Robert Darke kept an interest in the problem. He brought Clay together with an old school friend of his who was now a state legislator. After a weekend of successful hunting at the Darke ranch, and plenty of good food and drink, the friend introduced a bill to allow veterinarians to move more quickly against suspect animals.

The state acted on one of the commission's first

recommendations. Animal Damage Control, acting with health officials, conducted an experimental air-drop of bait containing rabies vaccine for coyotes. It was still too early to know whether it would be successful, since no one knew if the coyotes would absorb enough vaccine just by biting the bait.

When outbreaks in coyotes showed up along the lower Rio Grande and leaped north toward San Antonio and the hill country, the Texas Department of Health placed all 254 counties under a rabies quarantine.

And still no word on Jessica Rex.

Then, one morning in late February, Billy Deed came into the trading post and said, "Word has passed from the other side that she's in Juarez."

I didn't need to ask whom he meant by *she*. I threw down the months-old magazine I'd been reading and jumped to my feet.

"I'm going to Juarez now," Billy said. "Come with me? You and Clay?"

"Clay's in Austin. I'll be ready in ten minutes."

"Wear old clothes, so no one thinks we're the law."

We traveled in Billy's pickup. Tension kept us both quiet for the long hours of the drive.

Billy took the pickup across the international bridge and as far as he could maneuver into the narrowing streets of the *colonias* of Juarez. When the pavement ended, he parked the pickup, called over a boy of about ten from among the children congregated nearby, and paid him a dollar to watch the truck, with the promise of three dollars to come if it remained untouched until we got back.

"It's not worth my time, man, for less than five," came the answer. Billy handed the kid another dollar and agreed to five.

From there we walked along a winding dirt road past the cardboard, cinder block, and scrap metal shelters. The road served as a communal parlor where vendors spread their wares. Every necessity was for sale: utensils, vegetables, used clothing, car parts. Relentless noise swallowed up the air. The calls of vendors, the squeal of motorbikes, the barking of dogs, the chatter of pedestrians, the cries of babies. Children shouted as they played and rummaged in the rubbish in ravines where dogs scavenged. The dry wind picked up the gritty dust and carried it everywhere, stinging eyes and choking throats.

"I'm going to have to ask someone," Billy said, as we rounded a curve to find dirt paths spreading in all directions.

I pointed out a dusty Chevy van, one of dozens in Juarez that buses workers to and from the border factories. "The guy changing his tire over there will know."

The driver kept on with his work while Billy asked about the address we sought.

"I haven't had my lunch yet," he said. "I don't think I know that place."

Billy held out two folded dollar bills. "Let me buy you lunch."

Grinning, the driver pocketed the bills and pointed a grimy finger. "Down there," he said.

He was pointing toward a path marked with a

crudely lettered wooden sign that read AVENIDA CHA-PULTEPEC.

"At the end," the driver added, removing the jack and preparing to drive away.

We followed the path to its end and found a cement block building at the edge of the mesa where the pick-and-shovel excavations of the *colonia* stopped. Propped against the front wall a sign painted in black on a white vertical board read MÉDICO.

"This can't be right. It's a clinic," Billy said.

I suggested we ask inside.

Beyond the cracked glass door, patients crowded a ten-by-ten-foot waiting room furnished with a dozen molded one-piece plastic chairs in mismatched colors. A thin partition separated the waiting room from a ward of five cots. Another partition marked off an office or examining room where we could hear voices. We remained in the only available space by the front door, waiting. The patients, mostly women with small children or elderly people, eyed us without curiosity, resignation in their eyes. Presently a tired-looking middle-aged man in a much-stained white lab coat escorted a woman with a tiny, crying child out. As he held the door for her, he darted a glance at us.

"Yes?" he said. The word asked several questions. What are you doing here? Does it mean trouble for me? Are you city officials? Ministry of Health? Missionaries?

Billy introduced us. Explaining our purpose was more complicated. Seeing the hesitation in Billy's face, the doctor—his name, he said, was Luis Mendez—asked us into his office.

The room had a desk, two chairs, an examination table, and a wooden cabinet for the meager medical equipment and supplies.

The doctor invited us to sit, motioning me to the patient's chair and pulling the chair from behind his desk for Billy. He pushed aside a box containing a stethoscope, a blood-pressure gauge, and a pair of rubber gloves, and leaned against the edge of the beat-up desk.

"We apologize, Doctor, for interrupting your day," Billy said, "but we're looking for someone, a woman—"

"Her name is Jessica Rex, though she might be going by another name. She's white, tall, blonde hair, late twenties," I said.

"Jessica Rex," Doctor Mendez repeated as if committing the words to memory. "Are you a relative?" He looked at me.

"I'm an acquaintance," I said, watching his face for more information, wondering how much he knew.

"Not a friend?"

"No," I answered. "Not a friend. She was staying as a guest in our area when she disappeared. If she's here, we'd very much like to talk to her."

The doctor rubbed sensitive-looking fingers across the stubble on his chin. "I'm sorry," he said, looking back and forth between Billy and me. "The woman died this morning."

Billy jumped to his feet. "Can you prove it?" he asked.

The doctor paused, shocked, judged Billy's face, and found whatever answer he searched for. He crossed to the door and said, "Follow me." He went through the waiting room, past the cots, out a rear door, and across a scorched-earth yard toward a shed. At the door of the shed he stopped and faced us.

"Two people," he said, "a man and a woman, brought this woman here four days ago. They gave me no names. As you might guess, I don't ask questions in such cases. They claimed to have found her on the streets. Already she was beyond my help. It was a mercy when she slipped into a coma."

Probably a car-pedestrian accident, I thought. The most conscientious Mexican citizen, drivers and witnesses, will flee the scene of any accident, since remaining on the scene means going to jail until the Mexican police decide they have all pertinent information. And that means until the necessary bribes have been paid. For an American, it can mean more money than a tourist carries in his wallet. The couple that had carried Jessica here had done more than many would have.

Doctor Mendez used a key to open the padlock and pushed the flimsy door open. The shed was cement-floored, dark and dusty. A tarp covered the long table. A sheet had been draped over a contorted form on top of the tarp.

"Can I see her?" Billy said. "I must be sure it's the right person."

"It was a hard death," Doctor Mendez said. He folded the sheet back from the face. I took one look and turned away. Billy stood tight-lipped and staring.

"The rigor will pass," the doctor said. "Sometimes it sets in instantly when the person dies in great distress."

I tried to think of other things. Billy was taking deep breaths. The doctor covered Jessica's face.

"Does she have family?" he asked.

"No," I said. "After she disappeared, her father had a second massive stroke. He died last week. I think burial here in Juarez would be best. If you could arrange things, Doctor Mendez, I'll take care of the expenses."

He nodded. "You're wise to have her buried here. Getting a U.S. citizen's body out of my country can be very costly. Here, a few thousand pesos to take care of the necessities..." He shrugged his shoulders. Everyone, he seemed to be saying, knew the health officers, the undertakers, and the grave diggers would accept a bribe to move things along. It was expected.

"Let's go outside," I said. We waited while he secured the door.

"What happened to her?" Billy asked.

"She had rabies," the doctor said. "I found the scar from the bite on her ankle. A dog bite is my guess, from the marks. Or maybe a coyote."

"A dog," I said.

The doctor looked at me, but didn't question how I knew. "I see too many cases of rabies in humans," he said. "Though it's not so common a cause of death as malnutrition, diarrhea, and tuberculosis. I fight ignorance and superstition as much as disease. They go to the *curanderos* or the witches first. Only when they get desperate do they come to me. Usually too late. I fill out more certificates of death than certificates of birth."

I got out my billfold and gave the doctor enough

in pesos to cover his expenses, plus money for the funeral.

"This is too much," he said, trying to hand some back.

I shook my head. "For the clinic," I told him.

"Then, thank you," he said.

He walked with us around the clinic building to the front. We said good-bye and left him to go back to his patients.

"Ironic, isn't it," Billy said, as we walked, "that she died like that. It was White Dog, don't you think, that bit her?"

"I think so, because of what Linden told us." I stopped and stared back at the clinic. "Doña Aurora predicted this," I said, speaking more to myself than to Billy.

"Predicted what?" he asked.

"That there would be one more death. I thought maybe it was Trinidad's death she foresaw. But I think, now, this must be the death she meant."

We walked on and reached the pickup. The guard boy was sitting on the tailgate, kicking his feet and singing at the top of his lungs a border ballad about love, bravery, and sacrifice. Billy handed over the three dollars owed. Cash in hand, the boy jumped off the tailgate and ran through a nearby doorway. I stood waiting for Billy to unlock the pickup and take the antitheft device off the steering wheel, idly watching to see if the boy would come out again. In the shadow of the doorway, a tall thin figure of a man raised a hand in greeting before stepping back. Although Luke Fair was not wearing his lucky hat, I recognized him. Now I knew who had sent word to Billy about where Jessica was. Living here, Luke would naturally know everything that happened. Word passes.

I climbed into the pickup. I didn't say anything to Billy. If Luke had wanted to be known, he'd have come forward.

Billy started the motor and backed up carefully until he could turn.

"Do you think the doctor makes even survival income running that clinic?" I asked.

"If he's lucky," Billy said, "he might get ten dollars a day. No matter how small the fee he charges, I doubt that more than half his patients can pay."

"He could use some equipment."

"A sterilizer for starters. And disposable needles."

"I think I know what we should do with the reward from the lawyers."

A check for five thousand dollars had arrived three weeks after I mailed Rhea's documents to the lawyers for the fourth Mrs. Rex. Accompanying the check was a letter expressing the gratitude of their client after the judge had ruled her marriage to King Rex invalid due to a previous and still valid marriage to Rhea Fair. I had tried to give the money to Billy, but he had refused it.

Billy mulled over my suggestion for a few miles, then said, "Mother and Dad would have liked that."

That settled, I sat back and watched the miles speed past. It would be dark before we reached home. In a few hours I would spell Billy at the wheel. I stole a glance at his grim face. He needed a good meal, hot coffee, and rest. For months he had anguished over the murders of his parents, then for almost three months over the escape of their killer. Now he had to face the emptiness of his loss.

As the timeless desert turned golden with the sunset and then blue-violet with the night, I reflected on everything that had happened. I had gone looking for Rhea's killer and found the person who murdered my best friend. While I thought I was exacting justice, fate had already ordained Jessica's death. White Dog had killed the woman who had killed his mistress. All Jessica's plans and intentions had been lost in the instant it took the dog to bite her. And that before she ever knew my name. So much for playing Nemesis.

Would I do it again? You bet.

EPILOGUE

LATE ON A windless July day so hot you could smell the scorched earth, I drove to the post office to pick up the mail.

The shade of the cottonwoods in front of the Ramos's adobe dropped the three-digit reading on the thermometer only a few degrees, but that was inviting enough to draw several people to sit and visit on the porch. I stepped over Lucy's dog, asleep in front of the door, and went inside and emptied my box. Two catalogs, one letter.

I looked curiously at the slightly dirty envelope. The printed address read: La Señora, The Trading Post, El Polvo, Texas. The zip had been written in by a postal clerk. There was no return address. Postmarked Dallas, the letter had been mailed in May.

I tore it open at one end and tipped out the contents—a piece of paper, wilted and creased. With care, I unfolded it, gasped, then laughed with delight.

In my hand I held a familiar page torn from a magazine and picturing a color photograph of the skyline of Dallas lighted for Christmas. Across the page, written in black marker were the words: *"¡Yo estoy aquí!"*

"I am here!"

FREE BOOK OFFER!

Dear Reader,

Thank you for reading this Worldwide Mystery™ title! Please take a few moments to tell us about your reading preferences. When you have finished answering the survey, please mail it to the appropriate address listed below and we'll send you a free mystery novel as a token of our appreciation! Thank you for sharing your opinions!

1. How would you rate this particular mystery book?

   1.1 ❑ Excellent   .4 ❑ Fair

    .2 ❑ Good   .5 ❑ Poor

    .3 ❑ Satisfactory

2. Please indicate your satisfaction with The Mystery Library™ in terms of the editorial content we deliver to you every month:

   2.1 ❑ Very satisfied with editorial choice

    .2 ❑ Somewhat satisfied with editorial choice

    .3 ❑ Somewhat dissatisfied with editorial choice

    .4 ❑ Very dissatisfied with editorial choice

Comments _____

_____(3, 8)

3. What are the most important elements of a mystery fiction book to you?

_____

_____(9, 14)

4. Which of the following types of mystery fiction do you enjoy reading? (check all that apply)

  15 ❑ American Cozy (e.g. Joan Hess)

  16 ❑ British Cozy (e.g. Jill Paton Walsh)

  17 ❑ Noire (e.g. James Ellroy, Loren D. Estleman)

  18 ❑ Hard-boiled (male or female private eye) (e.g. Robert Parker)

  19 ❑ American Police Procedural (e.g. Ed McBain)

  20 ❑ British Police Procedural (e.g. Ian Rankin, P. D. James)

5. Which of the following other types of paperback books have you read in the past 12 months? (check all that apply)

  21 ❑ Espionage/Spy (e.g. Tom Clancy, Robert Ludlum)

  22 ❑ Mainstream Contemporary Fiction (e.g. Patricia Cornwell)

  23 ❑ Occult/Horror (e.g. Stephen King, Anne Rice)

  24 ❑ Popular Women's Fiction (e.g. Danielle Steel, Nora Roberts)

25 ❑ Fantasy (e.g. Terry Brooks)
26 ❑ Science Fiction (e.g. Isaac Asimov)
27 ❑ Series Romance Fiction (e.g. Harlequin Romance®)
28 ❑ Action Adventure paperbacks (e.g. Mack Bolan)
29 ❑ Paperback Biographies
30 ❑ Paperback Humor
31 ❑ Self-help paperbacks

6. How do you usually obtain your mystery paperbacks?
   (check all that apply)
32 ❑ National chain bookstore (e.g. Waldenbooks, Borders)
33 ❑ Supermarket
34 ❑ General or discount merchandise store (e.g. Kmart, Target)
35 ❑ Specialty mystery bookstore
36 ❑ Borrow or trade with family members or friends
37 ❑ By mail
38 ❑ Secondhand bookstore
39 ❑ Library
40 ❑ Other _____(41, 46)

7. How many mystery novels have you read in the past
   6 months?
   Paperback _____ (47, 48)   Hardcover _____ (49, 50)

8. Please indicate your gender:
51.1 ❑ female   .2 ❑ male

9. Into which of the following age groups do you fall?
52.1 ❑ Under 18 years   .4 ❑ 35 to 49 years
  .2 ❑ 18 to 24 years   .5 ❑ 50 to 64 years
  .3 ❑ 25 to 34 years   .6 ❑ 65 years or older

*Thank you very much for your cooperation! To receive your free
mystery novel, please print your name and address clearly and
return the survey to the appropriate address listed below.*

Name: _____

Address: _____City: _____

State/Province: _____ Zip/Postal Code: _____

In U.S.: Worldwide Mystery Survey, 3010 Walden Avenue,
P.O. Box 9057, Buffalo, NY 14269-9057
In Canada: Worldwide Mystery Survey, P.O. Box 622,
Fort Erie, Ontario L2A 5X3

098 KGU CJP2   WWWD98G2